SLEEPING DOGS

SLEEPING DOGS

DOGS ED GORMAN

THOMAS DUNNE BOOKS

ST. MARTIN'S MINOTAUR

NEW YORK

This is a work of fiction. All of the characters, organizations, and events portrayed in this novel are either products of the author's imagination or are used fictitiously.

THOMAS DUNNE BOOKS.
An imprint of St. Martin's Press.

www.thomasdunnebooks.com
www.minotaurbooks.com

Design by Dylan Rosal Greif

Library of Congress Cataloging-in-Publication Data

Gorman, Edward.
    Sleeping dogs / Ed Gorman. — 1st ed.
        p. cm.
    ISBN-13: 978-0-312-36784-8
    ISBN-10: 0-312-36784-8
    1. Political fiction.   I. Title.
    PS3557.O759S63 2008
    813'.54—dc22   2007051733

First Edition: April 2008

10 9 8 7 6 5 4 3 2 1

To Kevin and Kate McCarthy

ACKNOWLEDGMENTS

Thanks to Julie Hyzy for her help with the Chicago material.

And, as always, thanks to Linda Siebels for her tireless work on my manuscript.

Every morning, to earn my bread,
I go to the market where lies are bought.
Hopefully
I take up my place among the sellers.

— BERTOLT BRECHT

Politics is a form of high entertainment and low comedy. It has everything. It's melodramatic, it's sinister and it has wonderful villains.

— RICHARD CONDON

SLEEPING DOGS

That morning two things happened right away. Chicago had a freak October snowstorm, and Phil Wylie, the man I'd replaced, was in the news. He'd committed suicide the night before.

The staffers up front were gathered in small groups. This was the headquarters for Reelect Senator Nichols, usually a busy and happy place.

It was obvious that Wylie had had a lot of friends here. The mourning, among men and women alike, charged the air with grief.

The staffers closest to the senator had joined him along with Mayor Daley for a breakfast saluting five men and women who'd once been drug addicts but who had managed to go three years without hitting up. Noble as it was, this kind of tribute always strikes me as cynical. This is exactly the kind of presentation politicians, even the good ones, choose for photo ops, as if it were something they did that lent these people the courage and determination they needed to handle their new lives so well.

I was happy to be here, in the private office reserved for the chief staffers. I was the paid bogeyman, as the media had come to privately call all political consultants. That is one reason we stay away from cameras and microphones. Our presence just reminds reporters of how much campaign cash flows to various kinds of advisers, gurus, visionaries, and snake charmers. We've come a long way from Abe Lincoln, who wrote his own speeches on the backs of envelopes, no doubt about that.

I read the *Trib* and the *Sun-Times* on my computer. I also checked the log to see if we'd been mentioned on any of the local or regional TV or radio newscasts the previous evening. We had, but it was routine stuff—as were the mentions in the newspapers—so I went right on to see how the fund-raising was going.

The race was tightening. Jim Lake, our opponent, had once been dismissed as a histrionic nut job. But apparently he'd gone to sanity school recently. He'd gone more mainstream lately—he no longer demanded that teachers carry guns in inner-city schools—and that had no doubt helped him. But more than anything, he was a powerful presence on the stump and on TV. He was a damned good speaker. Senator Nichols, for all that I believed in his politics if not in him personally, was an efficient but uninspiring politician. It was a problem for us. Phil Wylie had handled Nichols's two congressional campaigns as well as his first senatorial one. I still had no real idea why they'd split so bitterly six months earlier. That was when my own consultant firm had been brought in.

I was just finishing up my third cup of coffee for the morning— thank God for McDonald's drive-thru—when Doris Baines, one of the local staffers who'd been with Warren since the days when he was an alderman here in Chicago, drifted back and said, "I wish you could have known him. Phil Wylie, I mean. He was one of the nicest, sweetest people I've ever known." Her nose and eyes were red. She tamped them occasionally with a Kleenex. "Everybody loved him."

She wanted to talk. I pushed back from my desk. "Anybody have any idea why he might have killed himself?"

She shook her head obstinately. "That's the thing. We kept in touch—everybody here with him, I mean. Every few weeks we'd have dinner with him. He had a lot of friends—especially girlfriends—but lately he'd seemed pretty lonely. He had so much—he was so good-looking and so wealthy and he was always in the society pages for being at this gallery opening or this opera—" She started crying again. "But I guess it wasn't enough."

"I'm sorry I never got a chance to know him."

She started picking at her hands. Then smiled bitterly. "I remember what we all thought of him when Warren first brought him on. We thought he was this spoiled rich man. He drove a Maserati in those days and sometimes a Town Car would bring him to work. Those were in his drinking days. But once he got serious about working here, all that went away. He was just like the rest of us then—"

"With the exception of several million dollars."

A teary laugh. "Well, I guess you could say that. But you know what I mean. He worked harder than anybody else. He really believed in Warren."

"I don't think I ever got that story straight. Why'd he quit the campaign, anyway?"

Working her Kleenex around her eyes again. "You know, I've never been sure. The official reason was that they'd disagreed on some political issue. But they'd disagreed so many times before—they'd really argue. I have two brothers and they were like that growing up. Argue all the time. But there was never any doubt about how much they loved each other. And Warren and Phil were like that. So I'm not sure we ever got the straight story. All that mattered was that Phil was gone. Everybody always turned to him. He was like our older brother. He always knew what to do."

"Nobody tried to patch things up between them?"

"Teresa did. She'd gone to college with Phil back east. They were great friends. In fact, Phil introduced her to Warren one summer when they were all home from college. That's how far back they went."

Teresa was the senator's wife. Unlike many spouses of important people, she was not one who envied her mate the spotlight. An elegant woman who was nimble in public as well, she was much better on the stump than Warren. And there was a sweetness about her that I always drew on when the day had gone on too long or too angrily. A good woman.

"He was a lot like you, Dev. Sort of a disillusioned idealist. He still wanted to believe that people would come to their senses and do the right thing. Even the bastards, if you just fought them hard enough."

Kenny Lane, another staffer, knocked on the window that let us look over the entire front part of the onetime supermarket that was our official campaign headquarters. He waved for Doris to come out.

"Well, I need to get to it. We'll all be a little slow this morning, Dev. It's really a blow."

By now, and even though I'd never spoken to the guy, I was starting to get a little dejected about his death, too.

CHAPTER 2

✭ ✭ ✭ ✭ I put a gleaming silver fork into my rich red spaghetti. After my first bite, I hoisted my scotch and soda and said, "Raeburn, we're going to kick Lake's ass around the block tonight."

"My poor deluded friend. You'll be getting thirty sessions of electroshock after tonight. You'll be desperate to forget how bad old Nichols does. Did I ever tell you that he once put an entire stadium to sleep?"

"Uh-huh. Will these shock treatments come before or after your man withdraws from the race?"

"And why would he withdraw?"

"Because he can't take the shame of being on the stage with a man as superior as Nichols."

The place was the Italian Village in the Loop. My lunch buddy was Tom Raeburn, campaign manager for Jim Lake, our opponent. In high school we'd played basketball against each other. Only six months ago we had met up again when Raeburn, then a lobbyist for electric companies, had resigned his post to take on Lake's campaign.

Give Raeburn five thousand dollars to buy himself a custom-tailored suit and then watch the magical transformation that takes place. The moment Raeburn puts the suit on, it looks like something he bought at Sears for a hundred dollars. He's got the magic touch in reverse. He looks sweaty, disheveled, even a bit of a hayseed. Hard to imagine him in a room of sleek, gold-cuff-linked, tough-ass lobbyists trying to figure out how to slip the party in power a couple of mil under the table in the next year or so.

But I've always wondered if the seemingly guileless blue eyes, the almost juvenile way he laughs and tells jokes, and those moments when he just doesn't seem to understand something that's obvious to everybody else—I've always wondered if that's not part of a minutely constructed persona meant to deceive people into thinking that here's a rube they can run over at will.

Maybe the joke's on us.

"So how do you like living in a hotel, Dev?"

"I miss not having my books and my CDs, but other than that, it's not bad at all. Room service up until midnight. Maid makes my bed every morning and cleans up really well. I don't have to live in my usual hovel."

"And speaking of hovels, my friend, our internals are looking mighty good. While yours are more hovel-like."

"Hovel-like?"

"I don't suppose your internal polls show you how badly you're slipping, do they?" He said this ostensibly as a joke, but we both knew better.

"Shows us holding steady. Six, seven points."

"I have to remind you what that lead was less than a month ago?"

"That's because you muzzled your man. He hasn't mentioned being abducted by aliens lately. He was bound to pick up."

"I admit he can get a little out there once in a while, but at least he only takes his pee-pee out to screw his wife and to piss. He doesn't cast his seed over half the country."

"Warren's changed."

"Sure he has."

"I'm serious."

"I know you are and that's what's so sad. You can't admit to yourself that he's a serial fornicator. Does the name Bill Clinton sound familiar? You know, if Nichols could've kept his dick in his pants, he might have been your presidential nominee four years ago."

There was no disputing it. Despite the fact that he wasn't a great speaker, Warren Nichols was both handsome and imposing on the stump and in front of the camera. He had a manly charm that women loved and men were able to accept. Plus, he had, or so I believed anyway, a true sympathy for the people our system had long ago tossed aside. He'd come from great wealth, but his mother had managed to give him a social conscience. The summer right before the last national nominating convention, the two leading candidates had had the same number of delegates pledged to them. Warren was considered the alternative to both of them should the convention deadlock. But forty-eight hours after the press dubbed him a serious spoiler, his own chances were spoiled when a sixth-grade teacher's husband came forward and said that Warren had slept with his wife and that he had subsequently divorced her. Warren was lucky to be elected to his Senate seat. His presidential dreams were over.

"People change."

"You know, I believe that, Dev. I really do. I have a brother who used to have the worst temper I ever saw. His wife told him to do something about it or she'd leave him. He started seeing a counselor. He isn't perfect but he's cut it back sixty, seventy percent. People do change. I just don't happen to think Nichols has."

"You're ruining my lunch."

He smiled at me. "You think I spoiled *this* meal, wait'll you try to eat breakfast tomorrow morning. Lake's going to do so well tonight, you won't be able to eat for days."

CHAPTER | 3

I'd spent most of the afternoon in meetings. I needed to be alone. The light flurries that had swept into Chicago via Lake Michigan in the morning were now, by seven o'clock, heavy and relentless.

I was enjoying a one-person pizza and a beer in the parking lot of Wellington University, the Chicago college that tries hard to live down its previous rep for dumb rich kids drinking their way through four years of sex and mayhem. New dean, many new associate profs, several new endowments, and a public relations woman who was so good I was thinking of offering her a job in my political consulting firm.

I'd left the army after eight years of serving in the intelligence section, where I'd basically been a gumshoe reporting on suspicious people who seemed to have undue interest in various domestic military installations. Because my father had been a four-term congressman before his death, and because I had an uncle in the consulting business, I signed on as a copartner in a political shop. In four years we'd won five seats, two in the Senate and three in the House. We were attracting national notice these days.

Even back in my army days, I'd learned that if you wanted to be left absolutely alone, turn off your cell, park your car in the center of a huge empty lot, and enjoy your solitude.

I sat in my car in the parking lot near the building where tonight's televised debate would be held. Right now, with an hour to go before the stage was lit and the candidates took their places, the lot was almost completely empty except for a truck moving back and forth, with a rack of evil yellow headlights shining on its roof and a snowplow on its front.

Warren's campaign manager, Kate Bishop, had called earlier and said that there was something she wanted to tell me tonight. I was of course curious.

As the truck scraped the snow away, I reached over and took the small silver flask from the glove compartment. I'd been needing a lot more of this stuff lately.

Eventually the plow deserted this particular lot and I was left in the darkness, two drinks down and with the kind of pinpoint headache just above my right eye I always get when I have this kind of anxiety. Performance anxiety—Warren's performance tonight. It needed to be good.

I put the flask back in the glove compartment, I shut off the engine, I slid out of the car, locked the door, and stood for a minute, letting the snowflakes snap at my face like so many mosquitoes. The cold air redeemed me, chased a lot of my fear and most of my headache away. I felt one of those movie bursts of confidence where the hero shakes his fist at the heavens and shouts in triumph. Warren was going to kick Congressman Jim Lake's ass tonight in the debate. For one wonderful moment I was sure of it. Absolutely sure of it.

. . .

B ackstage was crowded with technicians, makeup people, and the staffers who'd come with the three newspeople who'd ask questions in the final segment. All of them on the move at one time. We'd been in the auditorium twice in the past thirty-six hours. I'd wanted Warren to get used to the feel of the stage, to his physical relationship to the seats where the audience would sit.

Lake was a crooked bastard and the errand boy for every mercenary corporation in the state, but he had the kind of table-pounding, self-righteous, easy-solution bravado that, kept under control, came off well on the tube. A man who knew his own mindlessness, as one pundit had recently noted. And Warren was going to expose all that tonight. The overnights would show that we'd picked up a few points.

Yesterday afternoon we'd spent two hours here, just Nichols and myself, going over the points that would most likely be raised in the debate. Instead of nerves, I noticed a kind of distracted quality in both his eye contact and his delivery. As if his mind was on something else.

A scent of sandalwood. A gentle hand on my arm. A whisper in my ear: "If I wasn't so beautiful, I just might let you sleep with me."

I kissed Kate Bishop on the cheek. She hadn't been kidding about her beauty. Hitchcock's gleaming blonde, that Grace Kelly upper-crust attitude that just missed arrogance. Tonight she wore a black sheath. Her golden hair was drawn back into a chignon. She was the world's most elegant single mom. She had a three-year-old daughter whom she kept under a nanny's lock and key. She'd been with Warren one term in Congress and during his first term in the Senate.

We were buffeted, jostled, bumped by streams of people rushing to get everything ready in the remaining forty-two minutes before airtime.

She was knocked against me. My arm went automatically around her waist to steady her and draw her near.

"Well, I guess we've both had our thrill for the evening," she laughed. "I'm going through the vapors right now."

"Me, too." Then, "So what were you going to tell me tonight?"

She put her soft lips to my ear, the scent of sandalwood arousing me not only to lust but to a strange kind of melancholy, and whispered, "I'm getting worried about Laura. The last couple days I caught her in the ladies' room really crying."

"Got any idea what's wrong?"

"No. But I think we both better keep an eye on her."

Then she took my hand and said, "Let's go see the lord and master."

Senator Warren Douglas Nichols had what looked like a lobster bib stuffed in his shirt collar. It was a piece of crinkly paper fitted so that none of the makeup being applied would get on his clothes.

His eyes were closed as the young makeup woman finished dabbing around his cheeks and eyebrows. He was a trim, good-looking man of fifty-six with the kind of Harvard virility Jack and Bobby Kennedy had. He was old Illinois money, the kind that made his great-grandfather a close friend of the most prominent men of his time, including the Wrigleys, the McCormicks, and the Searses.

"It'd help if you sat still," the makeup woman said gently. She was very young, very slender, pretty in a wan, wounded sort of way, a bit nervous and uncertain of herself when she had to give Warren an order. She wore an emerald-green sweater that set off her dark hair perfectly. And dark jeans that showed her slender body to be rich with soft curves.

Billy Hannigan, our chief speechwriter, and Laura Wu, our communications director, sat in canvas-backed director's chairs talking to Warren as we came in. Billy was one of the best speechwriters I'd ever worked with. He'd been able to give Warren a voice he'd never had before, a way of improving the presentation by choosing simpler and stronger words for Warren to speak. He was invaluable. And you could send him out to fix problems in the field.

Warren faked a frown and said in a mock unhappy voice, and more to himself than to us, "They're supposed to be calming me down, but all they're doing is making me more nervous. And now she wants me to sit still."

"We told him no sex jokes onstage tonight," Billy said. A black Irishman of twenty-seven, Billy was a Rutgers man and proud of it, as you could tell by all the T-shirts, sweatshirts, hats, and scarves he wore bearing the Rutgers logo.

"We also told him not to refer to Lake as 'my asshole opponent' for the first five minutes," Laura joked. She was a slender Asian beauty, usually confined in designer suits. She'd done undergraduate work at Dartmouth and graduate work at George Washington. Laura and Billy were both critical to the success Nichols had had in his first term.

Nichols raised a glass of Diet Pepsi to his lips, forcing the makeup woman to take a step back. Apparently she didn't want to get drenched if he got too wild with his drink. I wondered what she'd say to her friends about *us*. Probably that we were a bunch of overpaid wusses. And she wouldn't be wrong.

"Never get between him and his Diet Pepsi," Kate said.

Warren puckered his lips. Made a face. "The ice cubes have all melted down in this glass. Tastes like hell."

"See all the traumas he faces every day?" Laura said to the makeup woman.

Gabe Colby came in just then. Gabe was the policy wonk and second-best speechwriter we had. Given the long graying hair he wore in a ponytail, the collarless shirts, and the vests and the jeans that were his daily attire, you might guess correctly that he longed for the days of takin' it to the streets. He was one of those men of the sixties generation who believed that they'd never had a fair chance of turning our government into a utopia of acid with Jimi Hendrix images plastered on public buildings. He always smelled of cigarettes and sweat. It was easy to dismiss him as an angry, aging hippie, but the sorrow in his dark eyes was too vivid for tossing him overboard that way. I had no idea what the source of his grief was, only that it was a terrible burden for him.

"Hey, Gabe," Billy said. "Ready to see Lake get his ass kicked around the block tonight?"

Gabe wasn't a cheerleader. He just shrugged and said, "Sure hope so."

Kate and Laura patted him. One on the back, one on the arm. You couldn't watch him without wanting to help him in some way. But he sure was up on the issues. He could probably give Google a good run.

Warren set the glass down on the table next to him, then assessed himself in the large round mirror that road show actors made themselves up in. "God, I'm looking old. That's another thing that bothers me. Lake's ten years younger."

"Yes," Kate said, "but you're thirty years smarter. Once he gets off the subject of his support for the NRA, the antigay groups, and the talk-radio fascists, he won't have much to say."

"Do you suppose he'll be wearing his Nazi armband tonight?" Billy quipped.

"The senator here still won't go for my idea," I said. "When he walks out he breaks into a rap song and then lights up a joint. Get the eighteen- to thirty-five-year-olds."

"Hey, that'd be great," Laura said. "And every time he looks at Lake, he says, 'Hey, you my bitch.'"

Nichols smiled. "I appreciate you people trying to cheer me up, but I have to admit I'm scared as hell. I just wish I was a better speaker."

"You don't have to go out there and wave the flag, Warren," I said. "Just be yourself. You've got a good record, we're ahead in the run-up to the election, and Lake always overplays everything. That's why he scares so many people."

He sighed, waving his hand to silence me. "Lake's gotten better on the stump. You can't deny that." His gaze touched on every one of us.

"None of you will say it, but that's what's going on here. Even if we're ahead, I have to be damned good tonight."

"You've got to forget everything but the debate tonight, Warren," Kate said. "We didn't have this conversation. Nothing negative even entered your mind tonight. You're a handsome, articulate, manly, caring person who has a genuine need to help people who need help. And you know what's in this country's best interests and aren't afraid to stand up and say it. That's what you've got to remember tonight."

A sad smile. "I wish I could send you out there, Kate. You made me want to stand up and salute just then."

"All done," the makeup woman said.

"I should've introduced you," Nichols said. "This is Megan Caine, everybody. Billy tells me Megan is a registered member of our party and does work on commercials."

"Megan, you tell him he's going to do a great job tonight," Kate said.

Megan looked surprised that she'd been brought into the conversation. She even seemed a bit embarrassed. "Well, I'm sure going to vote for him. I don't trust Lake at all."

"That's what we need to hear," Billy said.

Megan opened her makeup kit and put away the pieces she'd needed to get Nichols ready for the lights and camera. "Well," she said, still sounding a little embarrassed, "good night, everybody."

We all said our good-byes as we watched her leave the small room, closing the door quietly behind her.

"Very nice woman," Nichols said. "I think she actually calmed me down a little."

He stood up in his starched white shirt with red-and-blue rep tie, blue suspenders, and blue suit pants. He walked over to the hangers and took his suit coat down.

"Ravishing as always?" he said.

"The ladies will be rushing the stage," Laura said.

"Well, as long as that includes my wife," he said. "I always feel better with her in the audience." He paused. Thought of something. "You know, I haven't had a cigarette in fifteen years but right now I'd sure as hell like one."

"You do good tonight," Kate said, "and we'll buy you a carton of Camels."

"Oh, God no," Warren said. "I know that if I smoked even one cigarette, my nicotine habit would come roaring back. I'd be up to a pack and a half a day in no time."

The knock. It could have been anybody at the door but we all knew better. Billy was closest, so he opened it. A man with a headset on said, "We need the senator onstage so we can get the final lighting set."

"Thanks," Billy said, closing the door again.

Nichols went into his breathing exercises. Deep inhalations, deep exhalations. He insisted that these helped, and if they did, I was all for them.

Laura stepped over and gave his suit coat a close inspection. Dandruff, dust, bird shit—who knew what she was looking for. But whatever it was, she brought her steely focus to the task.

Kate worked on his tie. There was a gap between the top of his shirt and the knot. She wanted to make the gap disappear and apparently it took some doing. He made a joke about her trying to strangle him but she didn't laugh. When work was at hand, Laura and Kate were heat-seeking missiles. All you could do was get out of their way.

"There," she said.

Warren directed his next words to me. "I don't make any weird faces this time, right, Dev?"

"Right. No matter what he says, you don't mug. You just stand there straight and tall. You're the adult. Leave all the drama to him." Lake was one of those pols who enjoyed eye-rolling, forehead-slapping, and premeditated frowning. All the time his opponent was giving his response, Lake was doing his version of a Three Stooges episode.

Unfortunately, Warren had started doing some of the same thing during the last debate.

"And I never use the phrase 'average American.'"

"Right again. Because that's a phrase he uses all the time. What I want you to do tonight is wait for him to use it and then say that there's no such thing as an 'average American.' That each man and woman in our society is an individual and should be treated as such. And that's why his proposal to suspend certain constitutional rights we have is so dangerous. Because we have the right to act as individuals, think the way we want to, express ourselves the way we want to, and he wants to take that away from us while pretending it's because of terrorism."

"You could knock him dead with that one," Billy said. "Even if he doesn't wear his Nazi armband, people will know what you're talking about."

"That's enough tutoring," Kate said. "Information overload. Now he just needs to get out there and relax and do what comes naturally."

"I love it when people talk about me in the third person—when I'm standing right next to them."

Kate stuck her tongue out at him. They exchanged smirks.

Laura took his arm and said, "I'll walk out with you, Senator."

"Well, I can't go wrong there, a pretty woman like you on my arm."

"I'll go with you," Billy said.

And Gabe said, "Me, too."

They left.

Naturally, I turned to Kate and said, "So you don't have any idea what's bothering Laura?"

"Not really. Laura keeps everything to herself."

"Well, I'll keep a closer watch on her. See if I can figure anything out." I glanced at my watch. "We better get to the auditorium."

She took my hand. Squeezed it. "God, I hope he doesn't fuck it up tonight."

CHAPTER 4

I once had a congressional client who thought I should pick out a comely maiden in the crowd and bring her backstage after the speech was over. You know, the way Elvis used to have his Memphis boys do it. I gave him a choice. I could function as his consultant or his pimp, but I couldn't do both such taxing jobs at the same time. He took my point but he wasn't happy about it. One day after he won the election he fired me.

I once had a senatorial client who took so many personal flights on corporate jets that his own staffers joked that he needed to register as a lobbyist.

I once had a congressional client who was a virulent supporter of civil rights but would not eat in a place where black people worked in the kitchen and would not shake hands with gay men for fear of AIDS.

They come in all shapes, sizes, and degrees of greed, lust, megalomania, pettiness, treachery, and—never underestimate this factor—plain stupidity. In other words, they're pretty much like the rest of us.

Sometimes you're amazed that a pol you've always thought of as a dreadful hack on the other side of the aisle will do something so noble it's breathtaking. Likewise, you'll see one of your own do something so cynical and underhanded, you're genuinely shocked and wonder if you know this man or woman at all.

Part of my job as a consultant is to simply babysit and hand-hold. The congressional staffs do the same thing. The more focused the public event, the more danger there is. Tonight I was wishing I'd brought a cyanide capsule along to put under my tongue in case things went badly. One tiny little bite on the capsule and I'd be out of my misery.

We were seated in the front seats, aisle right. Lake's people were seated aisle left. We all waved and smiled at each other, of course, resisting the impulse to flip each other off and then rush across the aisle and beat the holy shit out of each other.

Both groups were well-dressed, excited. They didn't hope to learn anything. They just wanted to see a career destroyed. The other fellow's. Of course. They wanted that single slip of the tongue that would forever paint the candidate as a clown. Fodder for comedians, pundits, and editorial writers. These were political gladiators up onstage tonight and they'd damned well better make it bloody.

A few of Lake's staffers glanced over at me and made faces insinuating that they felt sorry for me. That Warren was doomed. Not if he just stuck to the prep we'd given him. Staff and consultants alike spend hundreds of hours sifting through information from many sources trying to define a few issues that their man or woman can base a campaign on. Some of the time the issues are obvious. Other times you have to manufacture an issue. The other side is generally better at this because their voters like bombast. They can plug in to talk radio and pick up two or three issues a day. Our side likes to think of itself as more noble and sophisticated. Even if this is true, and it certainly isn't true all the time, noble and sophisticated can easily translate into boring. Think of our last four or five presidential candidates.

For all the prep we did with him, Warren was actually better when he didn't stick to the prep. When he spoke simply and directly and passionately about his beliefs. The problem was, once he got away from the talking points, he tended to wander and sometimes get lost. Time was a big factor—a sixty-second response in many instances—so he had to be concise.

I wanted to get up and pace. Sort of tough to do when you're sitting in a theater chair. I had a bad feeling about tonight. But then I had a bad feeling about every night. I suppose it's the consultant's version of flop sweat.

The debate was only a few minutes away, the audience packing the seats, the three journalists in place onstage and ready with their questions, and the microphones being tested and tested again. The atmosphere was that of a prizefight.

Kate leaned in and said, "I wish I'd gotten drunk for this." She was feeling the pressure, too.

"Just smoke a couple of joints."

She smiled and socked me in the arm. "Can you imagine what the press would do if I lit up a joint now?"

"They're just as worried as we are," I said, indicating the row where the upper echelon of Lake's staffers sat.

"If they are, they're hiding it better."

And that was true. Our half row of people was decidedly reserved, where the Lake people were laughing and grinning and jabbering away at people around them. They were treating this like party time.

Gabe was staring off. If he was interested in anything around us, he wasn't letting on.

The woman representing the university then walked to center stage with a hand microphone. She offered a pleasant, studied smile to the anxious audience and then went to work.

"I'm very happy to see that we have a full house for this very important debate tonight. I'd first like to thank the Wellington people for letting us use this beautiful new auditorium and for helping us bring this event to the public. They went above and beyond in making sure that we got everything we requested. And the same for state public television. They sent some of their best people here for three full days to give the candidates a chance to get used to the stage and the lighting and standing at the lecterns. The two gentlemen we're bringing you tonight are under a lot of pressure to do well this evening, so having the opportunity to be familiar with the physical setup is a blessing for all of us, not just the crew."

She moved downstage to where the three reporters were sitting at a long desk. Because they faced the stage, we could see them only by watching the big monitors suspended from the ceiling on both sides of the apron.

She introduced each journalist with abundant praise and then said, "Now let me present our guests for this evening."

They appeared quickly, resolutely, both of them swollen with fake confidence and toothy swagger, both blue-suited, hair-spray neat, red-white-and-blue happy to be here among the voters. They'd both likely peed their pants twice already.

The walk to the lectern went fine until Nichols stumbled when he was about three feet away from it. The audience gasped when it looked as if he might fall, then laughed when he not only righted himself but risked a courtly bow. He'd saved the moment. No need to put the cyanide capsule under my tongue just yet.

"That was really nice," Laura whispered to me.

"Oh, yeah," I said, "you can't underestimate the value of a good stumble."

"Oh, you."

The hostess kept the bios brief. Each man got fulsome applause from his side of the aisle. They stood firm accepting it, gripping the lecterns as if they were guiding a ship through turbulent waters. They knew better than to smile as their applause peaked. It would look too Hollywood.

The debate, though it really wasn't a debate at all, just a Q&A, began with the downstate reporter asking Warren if he regretted cosponsoring a bill that would have lessened mandatory prison terms for first-time drug users. "No regrets at all. If it's proved that they were merely using and not selling, then confining them to prison is a waste of their lives and taxpayer money. The prison population is too big now because of mandatory sentencing. Even the ABA has come to question the fairness of five-year terms for possessing a small amount of pot or crack."

Jim Lake, guardian of all that was right and holy, was quick to respond. "I have one question for my friend Warren Nichols. How can we be sure that a person is simply a user? Maybe all the police could *find* was a small amount. But maybe somewhere this person has a lot more than that. Maybe this person, unbeknownst to the justice system, is a major dealer. And maybe this person that Warren is so concerned for—maybe this is the same person who, allowed to walk the streets, will be the one who gets your son or daughter hooked on narcotics for life. I don't have to tell you what a miserable life it is for every family member when one of their own becomes an addict. I have good friends who are going through this very thing right now."

The fucker. I was against mandatory sentencing in most applications. But his answer had been much more dynamic and dramatic than Warren's.

And so it went.

The military, foreign policy, tax cuts, sex education classes in public schools, the influence of big business on Congress—you're always waiting for one of the journalists to lay your client out with a question so unexpected that you see, depending on how he answers it, a career hanging in the balance.

In the first twenty of fifty-five minutes, nothing extraordinary was asked or answered. They both were being given time to settle in, get more comfortable, so that as the hour progressed, they'd be better prepared to start laying the heavy-duty accusations and smears on their opponent.

The audience had been instructed not to applaud, so the candidates' voices were clear and distinct in the auditorium. The twenty-minute mark was reached, several more familiar questions asked, several more familiar responses given. Lake, a five-ten former Purdue running back and, unlike Warren, a very physical man, writhed under the constraints of politeness. His consultants had told him, as I'd told Warren, to start doing the drive-by shooting just about now. Lake was ready to blow up an orphanage if need be. All I could hope for was that his "opposition research" people hadn't come up with anything we didn't already know about.

Then I noticed Warren weaving as he stood at the lectern. At first I assumed his back was sore from standing so rigidly and he was just trying to loosen up when the camera was off him. But very soon not only was the weaving more pronounced, so was the way his head was angling to the right. He seemed groggy, like a prizefighter suddenly stunned by a punch from nowhere. He'd been hurt and maybe badly.

I don't know if I was the first to notice it or simply the first to make note of it out loud. The swaying got more pronounced. Whispers from the audience. Now he wasn't merely placing his hands on either side of the lectern—he appeared to be gripping it desperately in an attempt to stay upright. If I didn't know better, I'd say he was drunk.

"Something's wrong," I muttered to Kate.

And then another problem: He started slurring his words. Now he not only appeared drunk, he sounded it, too.

"What the hell's wrong with him?" Laura said.

"Shit," Billy said.

"Dev, you've got to do something," Kate said. And then she shook her elegant head and said, "Sorry. That was stupid. There isn't anything any one of us can do."

By now the entire audience was aware of Warren's problems. Not only was there whispering, there were also sniggers and the occasional outright laugh. Everybody was remembering the way he'd stumbled on his way to the lectern.

Lake started glancing over at Nichols with a kind of gentlemanly concern. He was playing it just right. Not scorn, not mocking, but alarmed that there might be something wrong with Nichols. *What a good and decent man this Lake is,* you hear Mom and Pop at home saying. *He looks like he's genuinely concerned.* No need for *his* consultant to pop a cyanide capsule in his mouth.

Stage left I could see the hostess appear for a closer look at Warren. Her body language said that she was as worried as we were. She glanced at the journalists.

"Senator," the Chicago newspaperman said, "when you first ran for this seat four years ago, you promised the voters that you would make certain that funding for special-needs students would be doubled if not tripled. But in fact in the projected presidential budget, it's been cut by twenty-five percent. Is that a major disappointment to you? And if so, what do you plan to do about it?"

There are moments in prizefights when you see that one man has no idea where he is or maybe even *who* he is. That was Warren at this point. His head was rolling around on his shoulders cartoon-style, his eyes were fighting to stay open, and one of his hands slid off the edge of the lectern so that he seemed to lose balance.

"Did he have a stroke maybe?" Laura said. I think we were all wondering the same thing.

The woman from the university reappeared and rushed over to him. And just in time. He seemed ready to collapse.

And here came the cavalry.

Lake quickly crossed the distance between lecterns and got his arm around Warren, lowering him gently to the floor. The consultant part of me thought: *This'll be on the Internet within fifteen minutes. And it'll generate thousands and thousands of hits within the first hour it appears.*

Lake played doctor, checking Warren's pulse, neck and wrist, putting an ear to Warren's heart, feeling Warren's forehead, apparently for fever.

People in the audience were standing now, trying to see what was going on up onstage. The monitors had been killed. There was no more laughter; instead, fear filled both sides of the theater. Death is something we all have in common. And right now everybody in the audience was terrified by its sudden dominion. Maybe he wasn't drunk, after all. Maybe he'd really had a heart attack.

Lake had never had a better moment. Even I had to approve of the way he whipped off his suit coat and balled it up to serve as a pillow for Warren's head. Even I had to approve of the way he gently raised Warren's arm for a second time and checked for a pulse again. Even I had to approve of the way he got Warren's shirt open and tossed away the necktie.

But my admiration was short-lived. I couldn't afford it. The man on the floor was my client. And no matter what it was that had felled him, the heretofore mad-dog opponent had gone out there tonight an also-ran and come back a star.

I tried to estimate in my rattled way how many points in the polls he was picking up. Two? Three? God, could he pick up five? And then when I saw what he was about to do, I had to wonder if he could possibly pick up seven.

Because he was about to perform—right on TV, right in everybody's home, right in front of God—CPR on Senator Warren Nichols.

No, he's not some full-mooner lunatic. He's a strong and compassionate man we can trust and have confidence in. No, I don't agree with some of his positions, but that doesn't matter when I've just seen what he's made of. He's the kind of guy you'd want for your next-door neighbor.

The only thing we were spared was the CPR. By then a real live doctor had run up the four steps on the west side of the stage and was tending to Warren. Was that a brief hint of disappointment on Lake's face?

Probably.

CHAPTER | 5

Ambulance.

Teresa Nichols rushed backstage from the audience, joining Kate, Laura, Gabe, and Billy as they stood next to the techs loading the gurney bearing the senator into the rear of the vehicle. Red emergency lights gleaming, stink of medicines from inside the ambulance, exhaust pipe propelling snowflakes into the darkness. Nose-freezing temperature. Winds that had already knocked down a lot of freestanding signage. Sand trucks now joining snowplows.

From what I could see when I got out there, Warren was either asleep or comatose. He showed few signs of life.

Teresa Nichols, a shining blonde who vaguely resembled an older Kate in certain ways, huddled under her fashionable blue winter coat and said, "I want to go with him."

The female driver nodded. "Sure thing, Mrs. Nichols. Let me help you up here."

Teresa glimpsed me over her shoulder. "I have your cell number,

Dev. I'll keep you informed from the hospital. I know you'll be busy here." Then she disappeared inside.

Kate, Laura, Gabe, and Billy escaped. I made a couple phone calls on my cell. By the time I reached the hall, a small lynch mob of reporters had gathered. They wouldn't bother to find Kate when I was at hand. I put up my hands as if surrendering and let their questions rip and tear and rend me with their imbecility. It wouldn't do any good to point out that they'd seen exactly what I had and thus knew exactly as much as I did. They insisted that I knew something I didn't.

"Have you been keeping any of the senator's health secrets from the public?"

"No."

"Does the senator like to take a drink once in a while?"

"That's not the question you're asking. You want to know if the senator has a problem with alcohol. The answer is no. And I'll save you some time—he doesn't have a problem with any kind of drug dependency. Period."

"Did you see him before the debate tonight?"

"Yes. And he acted fine."

"Do you have any idea what happened to him?"

"None."

"Would you agree that Congressman Lake showed people that he's not the crackpot your campaign has implied?"

" 'Crackpot' is your term, not ours. We've had and will continue to have disagreements over policy with Congressman Lake, but right here and now I want to thank him for all he did for Senator Nichols tonight. It shows that he's a man of great character."

I wanted to puke, of course. But that probably wouldn't have looked good to the folks at home.

Finally, the police got there and broke it up. This press conference, that was up to us. But it would have to be in another part of the building. For now, move along.

. . .

Twenty minutes later I was standing outside the back door of the auditorium letting the cold and the snow have at me. Once again the elements revived me. So much had happened in so little time that I hadn't had the chance to sort through it. The cyanide capsule was sounding better all the time.

The doc from the audience had been under the impression that the senator had suffered a stroke or heart attack. That was his first judgment. But as his examination continued he said he wasn't sure. He obviously regretted his first assessment. He'd not only looked foolish, he might even have left himself open to some kind of lawsuit. I felt sorry for him.

I thought through his second judgment, that he was no longer sure. But if it hadn't been a heart attack or stroke, what *had* it been? An aneurysm? I wasn't a doctor, I didn't even play one on TV. So my speculation was useless.

But being the cynic I am, my thoughts shifted from medicine back to politics. Not much doubt about who'd looked best tonight. There would be worry and sympathy for Nichols—despite the closeness of the race, he was a respected man in Illinois—but it would be Jim Lake who got the coveted John Wayne Award for the evening. The manly way he'd strode across the stage to grab Warren and keep him from toppling. The heroic way he'd helped the incapacitated man to the floor. And then—the sonofabitch—the way he'd returned to the stage (the cameras on him of course) and said, "I think we need to say a prayer here for a very good man we all have a lot of respect for. This isn't a time for politics, this is a time for joining together in asking God to spare the life of a true patriot and an honest politician."

The Internet. The cable nets. All the major newspapers. Slots very near the top on the evening news. And editorials across the land commending Congressman Jim Lake—who was happy to let pollution, global warming, racial discrimination, hate crimes against gays, ridiculous bank loan rates, and much more prosper on and on indefinitely—for being an example of what Jefferson and John Adams and whatever other boozers had in mind when they first got together to write the Constitution.

Tonight, a star was born. Phony as hell, most likely, but tricked up as it was, it had played beautifully for the camera.

Then I looked at it the way an army intelligence officer would in gathering facts for a report. Had it all been coincidence? If the audience doc wasn't sure it had been a heart attack or stroke, what had it been? What if what we saw onstage hadn't been an accident? This was politics, after all, and in the era of Karl Rove, just about anything you could get away with was the order of the day. (And the Clinton machine of personal destruction had been a good warm-up act to Rove.) So you had motive—to sideline your opponent and make it look accidental. And who stood to gain? Why, the John Wayne Award winner himself, Jim Lake.

Image: Warren in the dressing room making a face when he swallowed the Pepsi. He'd complained that it tasted bad.

Image: The young makeup woman dabbing makeup on Warren's cheeks, his glass of Pepsi very near her elbow.

Image: Chic Kate saying, "God, I hope he doesn't fuck it up tonight."

Behind me, her voice ragged with the cold and snow, Laura said, "We're going back inside, Dev. It's too cold out here."

Laura said to Billy, "People survive heart attacks all the time, Billy."

But something about the heart attack scenario bothered me. Bothered me a lot.

CHAPTER 6

I'd asked Billy, Kate, Gabe, and Laura to wait in the hall while I worked alone in the makeup room. Occupational paranoia had set in. You couldn't trust anybody, not even your closest staff members. They were privy to everything—our stands on issues, our media buys, our schedule, who we had waiting in the wings to endorse us, how the money flow was going, and, most important of all, if there was some whisper of scandal we were trying to cover up. And each of them had had the opportunity to be in here alone earlier in the evening. I wanted to check things out myself. But my search was a waste of time.

When I came out of the dressing room, I said, "Did any of you happen to catch the last name of the makeup woman?"

They each took a turn at saying no.

"Which of you got to the room first?"

Billy shrugged. "I guess I did. Why?"

"Was she there when you got there?"

"Uh-huh."

"Are you going to tell us what's going on, Dev?"

"Who was there, Billy?"

"Just her. The senator got there a few minutes later."

"How did she introduce herself to you?"

"Just said she was the makeup lady."

"Nothing else?"

He paused. "Uh, let's see . . . Oh, she said she was a big fan of the senator's and that she'd voted for him before and wanted to vote for him this time, too."

"And nothing else? You're sure?"

"I'm sure."

"We should be going to the hospital," Kate said.

"Good idea. You folks get over there. I'll be about twenty minutes or so behind you."

"I wish you'd tell us what's going on," Kate said. "Obviously you suspect something."

"I don't want to say anything until I've got a little more information."

One of the crew members walked halfway down the hall and said, "There are two detectives out here who'd like to talk to you."

"Thanks," I said. "Kate, why don't you talk to them?"

"They'll want to know about today. How he was acting and everything. You saw him a lot more than I did."

"I need to talk to somebody else. You saw what I saw. You saw more, in fact, since you were in the makeup room longer. And you're the campaign manager. You're the public face. And Laura's the communications director."

"We're going to lose this argument, Kate. We may as well give in."

"Thanks for speaking up for me, Laura. We all want to get to the hospital as soon as possible. Teresa has my cell number. You heard her. She'll keep in touch."

"Yeah," Billy said, "but that doesn't mean that you'll tell us anything she said."

"Let's get going," I said.

I walked to the opposite end of the hall and took a short staircase down to the main floor. I was looking for the woman who'd seemed to be in charge of the event. I remembered seeing a line of glassed-in offices to the right of the stage.

She was on the phone when I walked in. She was saying, with strained patience, "I don't know anything more than I've told you. I don't want to be quoted as saying it was a stroke or heart attack, because I don't know for sure what it was." She signaled for me to take a chair in front of her desk. "Of course he wasn't drunk." Pause. "Everybody saw what happened onstage. He obviously had some kind of medical problem that I can't speak to. If you want that kind of information, you should call the hospital." Pause. "It's not my problem that the hospital won't release information. He's probably only been there for ten minutes or so. Now, I'm really busy, all right?"

As she hung up, she said, "God. I'm beginning to wonder if the idea of a free press isn't better in theory than in practice." Then she laughed. "Don't quote me on that. I'm all for a free press, of course. It's just when they start moving in on you—"

Her oblong name plaque on the desk read PAULINE DOYLE. She was probably forty or so, a few pounds overweight, with wonderful little teeth that gleamed when her full lips parted. In her dramatic dark blue dress with a slash of lighter blue stretching from the left shoulder to the right hip, she was definitely in the desirable category.

After I introduced myself, she said, "Any word on the senator?"

"Not yet."

"I couldn't believe it. No matter how you prepare for these things, you never quite know how to respond."

"You can't prepare for anything like this. I just hope he's all right."

"Would you like some coffee?" she asked, inclining her head in the direction of a Mr. Coffee.

"No, thanks. I just wanted to ask you about the makeup woman we used."

"Oh, yes. Megan, uh, Caine."

"Do you use her regularly here?"

"I guess I'm confused about that."

"Oh? Why?"

"First of all, I'd never heard of her before. But second, somebody in your office called me yesterday and said that you wanted your own makeup person and that this Megan Caine would be here tonight promptly at six-thirty."

"Does that happen very often? That people bring their own makeup person?"

"Depends. Some do, some don't. I wouldn't say it's common, but it's not unusual, either."

"And my office called."

She leaned toward me, her eyes apprehensive. "I hope I didn't do anything wrong."

"I don't suppose the person who called gave you a name."

"Uh, Frank something, as I recall. I didn't see any reason to write it down. I'm sorry."

"You don't have anything to be sorry for."

Her phone bleated. "Oh, Lord, it'll be another reporter."

I stood up and smiled. "I wish I could help you. And thanks."

Near the back door a couple of undergrads, girl and boy, clipboards in hand, worked along two racks of costumes from the theater department. Apparently they were cataloging what they had. I watched them as I approached. Before they wrote anything on the clipboards, they examined the particular garment extensively. Whoever had ordered the catalog wanted a lot of information about each entry. There must have been thirty costumes each on the long racks. They were both about halfway done.

"Excuse me," I said, "I wondered if you saw our makeup lady leave here a while ago." I told them who I was and said that she'd left some of her things in the dressing room and I wanted to get them to her before she left. I described her to them.

The boy, wearing a crew cut that would have marked him a BMOC back in '58, hadn't seen her, but the girl, an attractive but awfully thin twenty-something, said, "I saw her. She had some trouble getting her car started. She parked right behind the door out here, which, technically, she wasn't supposed to do."

"Fast getaway," the boy said, not knowing how right he was.

"Did you happen to look out the door and actually see her car?"

"Oh, sure. Rob here went to get us a snack. So while he was gone I went out on the steps and asked her if I could help her. She looked like a nice woman, actually. Very pretty. Probably just a few years older than I am."

"Did you notice anything special about her car?"

"Well, it was an old clunker," the girl said. "Really pitted out. The car was brown but the door on the driver's side didn't match. It was gray."

"Would you happen to mean primer?"

"I guess I don't know what that is," she said.

I explained primer to her.

"Oh, I see. Sure, it could've been that. Like it was ready to be painted. Though I sure wouldn't waste any money on a clunker like that."

"You notice anything else about her or the car?"

"Hey," the boy said. I'd pushed too hard and suddenly all three of us realized it.

"Why're you asking so many questions?" the girl said.

"I'd like to see some ID," the boy said.

I obliged him. "In case I'm a Russian spy?"

He scanned my license and then showed it to the girl. "How do we know you're really with Senator Nichols?"

"Pauline Doyle is just down the hall. You can go ask her."

Both of them lost their confidence now. I must have offered the right name.

Girl looked at boy, boy looked at girl. Girl said, "Well, she had a big sack in the front seat from a store named the Daily Double Discount. It's this kind of tacky little store over by Riverdale."

She surprised me. The makeup girl was very white, very middle-class. Riverdale was a grim place for someone like her. "I worked with an outreach program our class did last summer with poor black kids. The store was nearby."

This was about all I was going to get. I thanked them and started off to the lot where I'd parked my car.

Just as I opened the door and stepped outside into the whipping snow, my cell beeped.

Kate said, "They've got Warren in an examination room now. This place is a zoo with reporters. But one of the doctors in the ER told me that they were checking for a heart attack or stroke. But he also said they run tests looking for every possibility."

"I'm on my way," I said.

CHAPTER | 7

Kate hadn't been exaggerating about the press. I had to push, shove, even kidney punch my way through the pack to get to the ER registration desk, where a surly nurse said, after I'd introduced myself, "You better be who you say you are. Two of them—" Her eyes took in the phalanx of reporters, videocams, recorders, and still cameras that I'd just escaped. The only thing that stopped them from overrunning and sacking the ER was the lone and nervous-looking uniformed security guard. "Two of them tried to pass themselves off as interns. They were so stupid they couldn't answer the first question I asked them."

Now I understood why she was so surly. The press can be a juggernaut that can unhinge the strongest of people. They'd descended on this poor woman and undone her. Her face gleamed with sweat and her gaze was jittery and bitter.

Billy rescued me. He'd wandered here from somewhere down the hall. When he saw me he came over. The nurse looked relieved. "So he is who he says he is?"

"Yes. He sure is." Billy looked at the press mob now calling his name. They knew who he was. I guess they thought he was going to say, *Aw, let them come back and hang with the senator awhile.* Instead, he said to the nurse, "You'll have nightmares for six months about this."

She managed a smile. "This isn't quite as bad as when that alderman got shot. But close."

As we walked down the corridor to the room where Warren was, the hospital smells began to bring out my Irish fatalism. Irishmen (I wonder about Irish*women*) have two obsessions, sex and death, and not necessarily in that order. Maybe it's because we spring from the loins of certifiable maniacs, the Celts, those merry fellows who painted themselves with blood before charging naked into battle. Their war cries, this being documented by historical accounts, were said to be so terrifying that the Celts could take villages without lifting a sword. Their screams alone sent villagers running into the forest.

The hospital smells didn't create images of the Celts, but they did create images of what lay behind all those ER curtains. And the sounds augmented the aromas. The little girl whose temperature had soared to a dangerous number, crying out now in sweaty delirium, and her tormented parents standing next to her gurney, imploring the young ER doc to save her. The old man lifting spidery fingers to receive the hand of his middle-aged daughter, who knew he would never leave the hospital alive. The teenage boy sobbing through the fog of drugs and drink, not knowing yet that his reckless driving had killed his best friend.

Sharp stench of meds. Muffled words of nurses. The stray cry, piercing as a bullet. The quick ratcheting clamor of curtains being ripped back along metal rods.

Two security guards stood outside Warren's door. They'd already dealt with Billy, so all they did was nod as we went into the room.

Warren lay, eyes closed, pale and damp on a gurney. He was hooked up to two different monitors that beeped quietly and frequently. His wife, Teresa, leaned over the bed, gently touching the back of her hand to his cheek. On the other side stood Kate and Laura. Kate's lips moved in silent prayer. Gabe sat alone in a corner, his eyes downcast.

When Teresa saw me, she offered me her free hand. I took it and moved closer to her. "So far the tests they've given him don't indicate a heart attack or a stroke. They're doing more tests. But one of the older doctors stopped in and asked if he'd been throwing up. Which Warren did twice in the ambulance."

A young doc came into the room just then. Indian, almost delicate, pretty. She walked toward Teresa. I stood aside. She introduced herself as Dr. Ajeet.

"I consulted with two other doctors, Mrs. Nichols. They wanted to know what he's had to eat in the last eight hours. We've already got the blood we need for a test. It's in the lab now."

"I'm afraid I wouldn't know, Doctor. Kate might know."

Kate raised her head as if scanning the ceiling. "Let's see—we had lunch brought in to campaign headquarters from a deli down the block. He either had corned beef or ham on rye."

"He had one of those energy drinks around four o'clock," Billy said. "I was alone with him going over a speech for tomorrow."

"He guns Diet Pepsi all day," Laura said. "It's pretty much a joke with the staff that when the senator dies, he wants heaven to be one big vending machine with Diet Pepsi in every slot." She was smiling until she realized the implications of what she'd said. "Oh, God, I'm sorry, Teresa."

"Oh, c'mon, Laura, I know you didn't mean anything by that," she said, looking down fondly at the face of her husband. Teresa was one of those trophy wives who'd surprised everybody by being a woman of intelligence and compassion. And a valuable political asset. The men of Washington wanted to jump her and their wives wanted to count her as a friend.

"I'm wondering about the Pepsi that tasted funny," I said. "Right before the debate."

"So am I," Kate said.

We told Dr. Ajeet about the incident that Warren had put down to melted ice.

"That's very interesting," the doctor said. "We're already working on the possibility that he ingested something harmful in his food or drink. But we're considering many possibilities. From what we can see so far, Senator Nichols is in a deep sleep. His vitals are all normal."

"He's asleep?" Laura said.

"Yes. The same kind of sleep you'd get if you took too many sleeping pills. Not enough to kill you or do any permanent damage—hopefully not anyway—but enough to put you to sleep for a long time and then to wake up with a pretty bad hangover." She turned to Teresa. "Remember, when we first examined him, Mrs. Nichols, we were able to get him to open his eyes and talk a little. That's certainly something we can do with cardiac patients, too. But it's also symptomatic in some cases of drug overdoses."

"Then he'll be all right?" Teresa said, hope making her voice sound much younger, stronger.

"Well, we're more confident now that that's what we're dealing with, anyway," the doctor said. "We still want to run some more cardiac tests on him, but at this point I think we're going to be able to eliminate cardio pretty soon now."

Billy said, "He's snoring!"

And so he was.

We all fixed our eyes on Warren's face. The waxen look was receding. The eyelids fluttered, though they remained closed. And through his lips came a wet nasal blast that was almost violent. He was a master snorer, no doubt about it.

"Oh, thank God," Teresa said, clutching my hand again.

At this point I assumed that Warren was going to be all right, so my mind shifted back to the mysterious makeup woman. And to a man named R. D. Greaves, the dirty-tricks man Jim Lake had employed in all three of his congressional elections. And had most likely employed for this one, too. Tampering with the drink sounded like something Greaves would do. Lake was, after all, running behind with only three weeks to go.

"Are you leaving, Dev?" Teresa said. She seemed frightened by the possibility.

"I'm afraid I have to, Teresa. There's a lot to handle now."

"Me, too," Laura said. "I need to go out there and face down that pack of jackals. Kate had her turn, now it's mine."

"You want me to write something for you?" Billy said.

"Thanks, Billy. But I'm going to give them so little information we won't need to write it down." A sly smile as she said this.

"I'll stay with Teresa," Kate said. The two women had always been friendly, something you don't always see in political relationships. The wife threatened by the beautiful staffer. The staffer gloating over the long hours she got to spend with the candidate alone. But these two women actually hung out together, with Teresa, who could not have children, even frequently babysitting Kate's daughter.

"So you won't need me?" Kate said.

"No. But maybe R. D. Greaves will."

She knew what I meant by that. Billy and Laura were already walking through the door and hadn't heard me. Gabe stood up, silent as usual.

"Oh, yes," Kate said. "I hope you can find him and pay him a visit."

Teresa wasn't paying us any attention. She was too busy touching Warren's face with her hand.

"I'll call you later," I said to Kate and then went looking for Greaves, though I didn't get far. In my search for a side exit door, not wanting the press to see me leave, I was approached by a long, lean black man in a tan Burberry and a brown snap-brim fedora. He approached me with his ID in hand and a large public smile in place.

"Detective Richard Sayers. And I believe you're Dev Conrad."

"That's right."

"I just missed you over at the auditorium. I talked to the campaign manager, Kate. Very nice, bright lady. But I wanted to talk to you, too. See if you had any ideas."

"I'm not sure what you mean." But I did know what he meant. He wanted my opinion. He obviously knew there was a possibility that Warren had been drugged.

"I'm looking to see if there's any criminal angle here. Maybe the senator had a heart attack or a stroke or an aneurysm. But then there's the possibility that a bad guy slipped something into his drink. That would make this a criminal act. A lot of people thought he was drunk. I imagine that's just what the bad guy *wanted* them to think. If there was a bad guy."

"I can't disagree with you there."

He studied me with dark eyes that held no compassion for anybody unfortunate enough to belong to the human species. "You're a little rattled right now. And I don't blame you. But we need to have a sit-down and very soon. You know everybody who was in that makeup room tonight."

"I don't like the sound of that. You mean that bad guy is one of the staffers?"

"I'm not saying that. Not yet, anyway. But that's as good a place to start as any." He smiled with those big white perfect teeth. "I'll be seeing you around. You probably need to relax a little right now."

He nodded and walked past me, toward the front of the hospital.

CHAPTER 8

✵ ✵ ✵ ✵ "Freshen that up for you, friend?" the bartender
  ✵ ✵ ✵ asked.

       "Please," I said.

✵ ✵ ✵ ✵ As he mixed me another scotch and soda, he said, "Hope you don't have far to go tonight. That damned snow doesn't want to quit. I told the wife I might wind up staying here. We've got a cot in the back. Of course she thinks I'm hitting on the two waitresses." He was sixtyish, balding, and saddled with the kind of smile that would remind younger women of uncles and granddads. I doubted his wife had too much to worry about.

The Parrot Cage lounge sat across the street from a new three-story hotel, a hotel that offered suites pretty much like small apartments for travelers who planned to be in the city awhile. I was here because two of the newspapermen I'd called said that, so far as they knew, Greaves was staying at the hotel and doing a lot of his drinking at the Parrot Cage. I knew he had an apartment somewhere in the city but was told that when he wanted to celebrate something, he took a hotel room for a week or two. I'd checked the hotel. Not there. I was hoping he would end up here for a couple of quick ones before he went across the street to get into his jammies for the night.

"Well, I'm going to stick around for a little while longer, anyway. Hoping to run into an old friend of mine. Man name of Greaves."

The bartender's face cracked wide open with a grandpop smile. "R.D.? He's some character, isn't he?"

"Oh, you know him?"

"Well, not know him, know him. But he's been coming in here the last three weeks. He likes it when the gal comes in to play the piano onstage. Always giving her money to play songs he can sing along with. He's got a hell of a good voice, you know that?"

"No. I guess I didn't."

The stage was not much bigger than a walk-in closet, and even that space was halved by the shiny new electric piano. The bar was on the west wall, small tables on the left. There were only three other customers, a black man in a gray suit five stools away from me and a thirty-ish couple who laughed a lot. It was a middle-class bar for salespeople who traveled and imbibed. I couldn't find a single physical reference to parrots. Maybe the urinals were shaped like them.

"Plus he'll buy two, three rounds a night for people. Usually scores with the ladies, too. Of course, they're not the little chickadees we'd all like to score with. He gets the middle-aged ones. But nice middle-aged if you know what I mean."

The black gentleman raised his empty glass. The bartender went to fill it.

A good singing voice, rounds for everybody, a better class of women in his lonely bed. This was unfortunate information to have because it gave R.D., the prick, a humanity I didn't think he deserved.

Where did you start with R.D.? There were some who insisted that he didn't exist. The reasoning went that nobody that corrupt and mercenary could possibly avoid prison as long as R.D. had. Then there were those who half-believed that R.D. was some kind of supernatural force. Nobody human could be as devious, as ruthless, as merciless as R.D. Just wasn't possible, the human genome being what it was. He had to be some kind of satanic being.

Item: Two election cycles back, Greaves paid sixty elderly black people to help pass out flyers that claimed that the sitting candidate had once been arrested for beating a black man so severely the man had been in the hospital for three weeks. Greaves had one of his techies Photoshop an arrest warrant that detailed the charge. He repeated this in four different cities and towns in the congressional district. This, along with equally dishonest direct mail pieces and truly inflammatory radio spots, helped suppress the black vote and contributed significantly to the incumbent's loss.

Item: The somewhat mannish wife of a sitting governor became the focal point of flyers that claimed that, as a NOW member, she saw nothing wrong with lesbians being gym teachers and touching girls and even watching them shower. The wife was Photoshopped holding hands with another unidentified woman. This was another candidate who lost his seat partly due to Greaves's cunning. His wife, heterosexual from all accounts, was said to still be suffering from acute depression, blaming herself for her husband's loss.

Item: Greaves hired a hacker to obtain the private medical records of an opponent. The senatorial candidate had suffered a severe breakdown following the death of his younger brother in a boating accident. This had been back in the Vietnam era. According to Greaves, the candidate used his brother's death and his own depression (which included shock treatments) to get out of being drafted, "the way too many rich boys were able to avoid that terrible war." The candidate broke down one night at a press conference trying to explain what the loss of his brother had meant to him. The raw emotional display helped lose him the election. Too unstable.

Probably the most explosive charge Greaves had ever concocted dealt with a congressman who'd developed a rare blood disease and lost thirty pounds in a five-month period. Sounds like AIDS to me, the flyers said.

And the push calls, too, those phone calls that start out by claiming they're doing an independent survey and need only about sixty seconds of your time. In this case the second or third question of four was: Would you vote for a congressman if you knew he had contracted the AIDS virus? Hundreds of these calls were made in the final two weeks of that election cycle. And they worked perfectly.

Make no mistake. Neither side can claim virtue. Just about any election you can point to is dirty on both sides in some way, from teenagers tearing down the yard signs of your opponent to shouting down the man or woman who is trying to speak to a crowd. It's a matter of degree. Both sides, at the congressional level all the way up to the White House, have their election assassins. And both sides have done a lot of sleazy and unforgivable things to the election process. But only one side ever fielded anybody like R. D. Greaves.

"I'm going to be closing up pretty quick here," the bartender said after walking to the front window and taking a look at the parking lot. "Doesn't show any signs of letting up."

"Give me one more while I visit the john."

"Sure thing."

And when I got back, he was there. R. D. Greaves himself. Sitting at the far end of the bar where the black gentleman had been.

He didn't recognize me. I took my seat and started working on my fresh drink. During my brief sojourn in the john, the other customers had left. Now it was just the three of us.

The bartender looked confused. He must have thought that I'd be sitting up close to Greaves, since I'd told him we were old friends. He finally said, as he wiped out a glass with a towel he should have tossed about twenty glasses ago, "R.D., man down there's been asking about you."

I suppose the bartender thought that this introduction would end in some kind of beer commercial backslapping by two big manly men. *Hey, shit, I didn't recognize you! How the hell you been, man? Let's us have a brewski!*

But all that happened was that Greaves turned a bit on his stool and glared down the bar at me and said, "Is that right? He tell you *why* he's been asking about me?"

Greaves and I are both shaggy mastodons. Six-four or thereabouts, noses broken a few times by those snobs who found us less than charming, waistlines that had to be carefully watched, and the ready anger that shrinks would probably call paranoia. He wasn't physically afraid of me and I wasn't physically afraid of him. The bartender clearly sensed this and as a result started looking nervous.

"So why're you asking the barkeep so many questions?"

"I thought maybe he could tell me if you were really as big a prick as people say you are."

Now in your standard cop or cowboy movie, those would be fightin' words. The stuntmen would double the actors and a furniture-bustin' brawl would ensue. But this, alas, was reality, and men our age and our size had to be careful about brawls. Even in your early forties, you didn't recover from physical violence the way you once might have.

He laughed. Or rather, bellowed. "Hell, yes, I'm a big prick. Probably more than you even heard. So who the fuck are you?"

"Campaign consultant to Senator Nichols."

All he said was, "Figures." Then he turned around and faced the mirror again. He shoved his empty glass at the bartender. "Hit me again, Mike."

I slid off my stool and slowly made my way up the bar. Mike looked to be quietly hyperventilating.

"I suppose you heard about tonight. The debate?"

He didn't turn to look at me. "Was there a debate tonight? Guess I didn't hear about it."

"Somebody put something in my client's drink. Something that made him so groggy he passed out onstage."

"Man, sounds like I missed something. Maybe I can pick it up on a news show. That'd be some footage I'd bet."

"Sounds like something Jim Lake would hire somebody to do."

He angled around to face me. "I don't know anybody who'd do anything like that, Sport. We all have too much respect for our system of government. The whole election process is a sacred right. A lot of people have fought and died for it."

I didn't do it. Somebody else did. Somebody who looked an awful lot like me. I just stood back and watched as this doppelgänger smashed a right hand into the side of Greaves's head. Hard enough to knock him off his stool and onto the floor, where he cracked his head on landing.

Mike pulled a sawed-off from behind the bar and started shouting at me. "You freeze right where you are, mister! I ain't putting up with this kind of shit from anybody!"

Carefully keeping both barrels pointed in my direction, Mike came out from around the bar to see how Greaves was doing.

Greaves was doing just fine. Picking himself up, straightening his clothes, touching his fingers tentatively to the spot where my fist had collided with his face.

"You want me to call the cops, Mr. Greaves?"

"Hell no, Mike. I was actually going to look this creep up anyway. He just saved me some time is all." He lifted his drink, draining it, "C'mon, creep, I'll buy you some food."

So that was how I met the one, the only, R. D. Greaves.

You know, Leno and Letterman are always making jokes about Denny's, but I like this place. The food's good and pretty cheap. I've never found anything in my food. You know, a finger or anything like that. And the booths are comfortable. You take Burger King, those are the most uncomfortable fucking booths I've ever sat in. You ever eat at Burger King?"

"Not unless my kidnappers forced me to."

He was shoveling ketchup-drenched french fries into his mouth one by bloody one as he talked. He had red streaks across his upper lip and on the left side of his mouth.

"So how'd you ever get into the political racket?"

"My father was a congressman. He got tired of seeing people like you working for people in Congress."

He winked at me. It was obscene. "Not to brag, but there's never been and never will be anybody 'like me.' Look it up. Nobody's got my track record."

"I'll bet your mother's proud of you."

"As a matter of fact, she's *very* proud of me. Brags about me to everybody in the old neighborhood."

"Figures."

He seemed to bring me into focus for the first time. He had the kind of Gene Hackman looks that could turn easily into good guy or bad guy. "You're a sanctimonious bastard."

"One of my many failings." And it was.

He ate some more french fries. He'd obliterated his cheeseburger in four Olympian bites. I was almost afraid to see what he'd do to the three-scoop chocolate sundae he'd ordered right along with his meal. It had been sitting here long enough to melt. "So you think I did in Nichols tonight, huh?"

"Pretty sure you did."

"What makes you think so?"

"(A) It's your MO. You get creative when you're down this close to Election Day. (B) The woman who actually dropped the drug in the drink gave a phony name and lied about being part of the Nichols campaign."

He snorted. Now he had ketchup all over his fingers, too. "You think a grand jury would buy that?"

"Probably not."

"But you're gonna go ahead and try to nail me for it anyway, right?"

"Don't have time. Maybe after the election. Sooner if I can find the woman."

He held a single french fry that drooped under the weight of the ketchup. Then he opened wide as if I were his dentist and shoved it into the darkness between his teeth. "It's funny, I don't even know who she is, never met her, never saw her, but I've got this feeling about her. Sort of a psychic kind of thing."

"Sure. Psychic kind of thing."

"I just have this feeling she got on a plane right after this thing at the auditorium tonight—she got on this plane and flew bye-bye. If she's any kind of pro, that is."

He was having some fun with me. Scatting. Seeming to pretend he knew something about the drugging while denying it when asked directly. He was good at confusing you.

"You think so, huh?" I said.

"I know so."

"Funny, I had the impression she was local talent."

"You never heard of local talent flying away somewhere till things cool off?"

"More coffee?" the waitress said.

We both said no but Greaves pointed to his sundae. "I didn't get to this as fast as I thought. How about throwing this one away—or giving it to somebody in the kitchen—and getting me a new one. I'll pay for it of course." He patted her hip. "Or you can eat it for yourself, darling."

She smiled. "I think I'll take you up on that. It looks good."

When she was gone, he said, "Nice ass but no tits."

"She should be killed for not measuring up to your high standards."

His last french fry got swished around through a large dollop of ketchup remaining on the platter. "You're an owly son of a bitch."

"The nuns always told me that, too."

"You went to Catholic school?"

"Yeah."

"Hey, so did I. But then one day it hit me."

"What hit you?"

"All this God shit. It's all a crock. When we die, we die. Same as when you see a dog or a cat that's been run over by a car. It's all they get and that's all we get, too."

"So why follow the rules when this is it right here on earth, right?"

"You're getting sanctimonious again but, yeah, that's right. I mean, what the fuck, may as well enjoy ourselves. You only go around once in life."

"That's a line from a beer commercial."

He winked at me again. "I take my wisdom where I find it, Sport."

The waitress brought his sundae. She stood away from him this time. She didn't want to be patted again. She dropped the check on the table and left.

He laughed. "Don't think I'll be waking up with her in the morning." He then proceeded to demolish his sundae in six skilled attacks. He had whipped cream on the tip of his nose. I didn't tell him. I liked him better as a clown. He made a big "Aaaaahhhh!" sound as if he'd just finished a feast so impossibly wonderful, complete words couldn't describe it. He crossed his eyes and peered down his nose. "Hey, I got something on my nose?"

"Yeah. Whipped cream."

"Why didn't you tell me?"

"Guess I didn't notice."

"You are some kind of asshole, Sport." He napkined off the

whipped cream and then sat back in the booth, spreading his arms out on either side. Something had changed in the eyes. They appeared to be a much deeper brown, almost black. And the jaw muscles were bunched now. This was the political assassin I'd heard about.

"Sport, you got much bigger problems than what happened tonight."

"I do, huh?"

"Yeah, you do. And you're sitting there thinking you're such a superior shit—smarter than me, slicker than me, marginally better-looking than me—the kind of guy who gets invited to all the parties with the pretty people. The ones who hire me but don't want me around afterward. You know, I've never been invited to a single inaugural ball? Or to a single congressman's office. Or to a single governor's mansion. And it was me who helped put most of these motherfuckers where they are today."

I didn't say anything. I wasn't sure *what* to say. His cold anger had the force of a punch.

"But I'm getting off the subject here. We were talking about you."

"Right. And that I've got a much bigger problem than what happened tonight."

He went right at it. "I have a videotape of your senator fucking the brains out of a hotel maid. Nobody knows I have it."

My response was lame and we both knew it. "The kind of technology today, you can fake anything."

"I hired the girl myself and now she's my witness. So don't give me any bullshit about the tape being fake. You know I've got the real deal."

"If you've got it, why not give it to Lake and let him leak it to the press?"

He tapped his right temple. "You really are a babe in the woods, Sport. I give it to Lake, he just considers it part of my job. He might give me a little bonus or something. I did this on my own time. I want a big payday. So I'm offering it to you first."

"How much is this big payday you want?"

The smile was novel length. He had dreamed of saying these three words all his life. "One million bucks." And then he said, "By noon, day after tomorrow."

CHAPTER 9

"You don't look so hot," Billy said the next morning when he found me in the coffee shop.

"Thanks. I needed to hear that."

As he opened his menu, he said, "What's that bruise on the side of your head?"

"I slipped and fell last night in the snow. A lot of people slipped and fell in the snow last night, Billy. It's no big deal."

I'd slipped and fallen in the snow after R. D. Greaves had punched me from behind as I was getting into my car. He not only wanted a million dollars, he also wanted revenge for me knocking him off his stool in the Parrot Cage.

"How we going to handle this, you know yet?"

I ate the last bite of my cheese omelet and said, "I need to get with Kate and Laura. If you mean are we going to charge Lake with putting something in Warren's Diet Pepsi, I don't know. This is the last thing you folks ever want to hear, but I want to see some overnight polling, see how people view Warren. That debate probably had a very big audience. Haven't seen any figures yet. But that would be my guess."

"I guess I don't understand. If Lake did it—"

Waitress. Billy was in a decisive mood this morning. "What'd you have, Dev?"

"Cheese omelet, orange juice, unbuttered toast, and coffee."

"Same except butter the toast."

When she went away, he said, "But we know Lake did it."

"We don't *know*. We *think* we know. There's a difference. Our only lead is that makeup woman, and the only thing I've been told about her is that she shops at Daily Double Discount."

"Never heard of it. And I grew up here."

"I've never heard of it, either. And I don't even know if it's a true lead. One of the college kids working backstage told me she saw a Daily Double Discount sack in the woman's front seat."

"Well, that's something."

"Maybe and maybe not. What if she'd borrowed the car or stolen it? And even if it was her sack, why would anybody at the store remember her? Presumably they've got a lot of customers or they wouldn't stay open long in the discount business."

"Oh, yeah, I see. But I still don't see why we can't call a press conference and sort of imply that Lake hired somebody to take down the senator last night."

Waitress with Billy's coffee.

"Because you can never be sure where an accusation like that will lead. It might look like desperation on our part."

"But we're ahead in the polls."

"We *were* ahead in the polls as of last night when Warren walked out onstage. I'm not sure where we stand this morning, though. And again, you and I are sure Lake is behind it all. But we don't have proof. And without it, it could all backfire on us very quickly. These are the three most dangerous weeks in a tight campaign."

"That's for sure."

"So what I'm going to recommend to Warren and Kate is that we hold a press conference sometime today when Warren is up to it and all we say is that Warren ingested some kind of contaminated food or drink last night. We'll have one of the hospital docs standing next to him when we say this."

"What if the press wants to know more?"

"We'll just say that we need to have more lab tests done before we can say for sure what it was he took into his system last night."

"You know they're going to be all over this story. He used to have a woman problem, but way back when, he had a drinking problem, too."

"Not much of one. He got into a couple of fights when he was in the National Guard. That's not much of a drinking problem."

"Yeah, but he was arrested once for public intoxication."

I'd thought the same thing during my long and sleepless night in bed. But by dawn I'd dismissed the "drinking problem" angle. The public-intox arrest was made when he and four other recent college grads set up their garage band out on the lawn of a vacated manse in the Gold Coast area. The movers and shakers of such a neighborhood were not at all amused by being awakened at four-thirty A.M. But he was twenty-one at the time and, as seen through the voters' eyes, who among us wouldn't want to cost those rich, selfish bastards some sleep? I still couldn't see the "drinking problem" angle that worried Billy.

"The staff's over at headquarters this morning," I said. "As soon as I finish up here, I'll be going over there."

"They did a great job on the streets during the night," Billy said. "At least we can get around everywhere this morning. Most of the snow is already melting. No Michael Bilandic moment."

Bilandic had been a briefly popular mayor who'd lost all his support when he failed to deal competently with a snow emergency. His administration's response was so lame that he lost to the then-unknown Jane Byrne in the mayoral primary.

"Warren's got three stops on his schedule today. He's going to keep every one of them."

"You really think he's strong enough, Dev?"

"He doesn't have any choice. We need to show that he's strong and can bounce back right away. That's another reason I don't want to make any accusations. It's more important to show that he's in charge of the situation than to put blame on somebody. They thought they could queer his drink and put him on his back for several days? Not our man. He's hitting the bricks the very next day. That's the signal we have to send."

Billy giggled. "It's like you're playing with toy soldiers, man. All you consultants are like that."

"That isn't a compliment. Not to me, anyway."

"But it's true."

"We want to win, Billy. And part of the reason we want to win is because we believe in what a given candidate stands for. I know that sounds like bullshit, but it isn't. I get pitched all the time by candidates I have no faith in and I say no. Elect these guys and they'll be in the pockets of every big-money lobby in Washington. Nobody's pure, Billy, but there are degrees of dirty. Our man Warren is pretty clean, considering."

Billy was smirking now. "Wow, I'm surprised. You actually do give a shit."

"Yeah," I said, "sometimes I even surprise myself."

I first started working in local politics when I was a sophomore in college. I did so for a simple reason. The pol I volunteered to help had some really fine-looking college girls working out of his campaign headquarters. I was hoping to get laid. While that didn't happen, my fascination with the political world took serious and lasting hold, mostly because of my father then being in Congress. I admired the pol I worked for because, even though he was a machine man, he didn't hesitate to veer from the party line when he felt it necessary. Pretty damned cool, I thought. And so did a lot of others. He got elected. And he singled me out for some suggestions I'd made to one of his paid staffers.

My reward was that I became a paid staffer when he was up again two years later. I did my work after my college day at Northwestern was done. Where before I'd done mostly phone answering, Xerox copying, pizza getting, and so on, this time I worked under the campaign manager, who was in charge of the finance director, the field director, the communications director, the scheduler, and the consultants. That summer I worked full-time, and it was better than a graduate program in politics. I learned the game and the game's most important rule: The first thing a pol generally does when he or she takes a mortal hit from the opponent is to fire the campaign manager. Announce that he or she is really sorry that such a mistake could happen (some real PR screwup most often) and that the campaign manager has been canned and a new one is on board and a fresh start begins right now. Campaign managers are well aware that they can and will be dumped at any moment when necessary. That's why they're paid well.

The second most important rule: Stay out of all the palace intrigue you find in campaign headquarters. There are endless rivalries for the candidate's approval and face time, hurt feelings, jealousies, even plots to get others fired. Human nature. The smart pol operative—which I already knew I wanted to be—keeps as far away from these follies as he can.

The Senator Nichols campaign headquarters was the standard battle zone you found everywhere with three weeks to go. Phones, faxes, copying machines, TV sets, cell phones, and iPods created a relentless electronic annoyance that you either adapted to or fled from. Some people can't handle it and quit. There were too many people despite the spacious floor plan of what had once been a supermarket. That was because the press was here today, en masse it appeared. They knew that Warren was in his office in the back of the headquarters. They were waiting to attack him.

I got myself a cup of coffee and headed back there, smiling, nodding, waving to people who smiled, nodded, and waved to me. The younger ones didn't much like me. Their poly sci profs had warned them about political consultants. People like me, they said, were responsible for candidates being prepackaged and bland and focus-grouped and polled to death. And unwilling to take any kind of stand that polls indicated might not be popular. And worst of all, their finale went, in the old days consultant services at least ended when the pol went to Washington. But now many pols kept their consultants on the payroll and wouldn't cast a ballot in the House or Senate unless the consultant approved it.

It always surprised people when I said that I generally agreed with these objections. And that I was guilty of some of those sins myself. What I didn't say was that the average consultant was much smarter than the average candidate.

I think Dev's right," Senator Nichols said half an hour later, after Kate and Laura had argued that we should at least hint that we believed Congressman Lake was behind last night's incident. He looked better than I'd expected he would and his voice was strong and persuasive. "Number one, we don't have any hard evidence. And number two, we don't know where an accusation like that would lead. Like Dev said, it might take over the whole election. The Chicago TV boys wouldn't let go of it. And the cable news people would go after it twenty-four/seven. Our message would get lost in all the drama. We don't even know where we stand today. I'm like Dev. I want to see some polling from last night before I do anything except stick my head out and say that I'm feeling fine, thank you very much."

Billy frowned. "Polls."

"Polls help pay your fee, Billy," Warren said gently. The top campaign slots offered some very attractive salaries. "And speaking of which, Kate tells me that we can expect a lot more money from the national party committee because of last night. They'll be getting it to us right away. They've suggested that we need two new thirty-second spots that show me strong and vital."

"I wrote them in the middle of the night," I said. "I have a production company scouting indoor tracks, handball courts, places like that. We can cheat a lot of the shots." I smiled. "You won't have to run more than fifteen yards, but we can make it look like you're doing a marathon."

Everybody smiled at that one.

Warren clapped his hands together. That always signified that we were done. "So if that's it, I'll let you all get back to work and I'll do the same here myself. I need to make some calls. And then about twenty minutes from now I'll go out there and face the jackals."

"You'd better," I said, "before they start bringing in blankets for the night. They might not want to leave."

Kate, Laura, Gabe, and Billy all said good-bye. Warren was expecting me to leave, too. He seemed surprised when I said, "There's a coffee shop down the street. It'll be busy right now, perfect for talking in private because everybody else'll be talking, too."

I tried to sound amiable but he caught the tension in my voice. "I have this place swept three times a week."

"I'd still feel better about us having coffee down the street." No matter how often you sweep an office, there's always the possibility that some new electronic spying gadget won't show up on your radar. If this office was bugged, all kinds of information would now be in Lake's hands. But nothing about blackmail and hotel maids.

"You're the boss," Nichols said. He tried to keep it light whenever he said that, but there was an edge of bitterness to it. We slipped out the back way and took the scenic route down the alley.

B ack booth. Place packed. Poor waitresses frantic.
    I said, "Hotel maid. Married man who happens to be a United States senator. Sound familiar?"

At first he didn't seem to understand. But then every feature on his face was suddenly dragged down as if by gravity.

"I thought you gave that shit up, Warren."

He made a fist. "That was a slip."

"Some slip."

"How the hell did you hear about it?"

"Courtesy of R. D. Greaves. He wants one million dollars cash for the video he has."

"Are you fucking crazy?"

"He says you come from big money. As you do."

"Not that kind of money."

"We pay for our sins, Warren."

Waitress. All either of us wanted was coffee. There's something about blackmail that curbs the appetite. We gave her our order then resumed talking.

"God, last night and now this? R. D. Greaves is scum. He must've planted a camera in there."

"Yeah. He did. And the girl was a plant. He has the tape, Warren. Adultery. Sleazy video."

"One million bucks. That bastard. I really think I'm going to start hyperventilating. No shit."

"Warren, we have to face this."

"I can't believe this." He shook his head three or four times. A fine sheen of sweat covered his face. "Have you seen the video?"

"No. But I will before we arrange for the money."

"How will you contact him?"

"He'll call me. He doesn't have any reason to hide."

"There's no way I can come up with a million. No way at all. Getting that much would cause so much suspicion we'd have the feds on us. And anyway, that kind of money is invested. Nobody would have it laying around in currency."

"He's given us till tomorrow afternoon."

"Well, I won't do it. I'd rather resign my office."

"No, you wouldn't."

"Shit." Then, "You're right. No, I wouldn't."

I said, "There's another angle here."

He smiled sadly. "With you there's always another angle. You work like a confidence man sometimes, Dev. Nobody knows quite what's going on except you."

"You'd know the same thing if you thought about it."

He shrugged. "Probably not. You've got street smarts, I don't. There's a downside to growing up privileged. You don't know jack shit about the real world."

The waitress gave us more coffee.

"I can tell I'm not going to like this," Warren said.

"You're right. You're not going to like this."

"You can be a real prick sometimes."

He'd spoken too loudly. The crowd had thinned considerably now that it was pushing nine o'clock. You could hear actual words instead of just noise. A couple of men in blue real-estate blazers looked over at us. They were surprised to see their senator. He usually had a body-guard with him. Right now he was just another guy.

In a stage whisper, he said, "You can be a real prick sometimes, you know that?"

"Here's the other angle. It's called honesty. When I signed on with you, one of the first things we discussed were all the rumors about you chasing women around. You said you'd given it up. Bopping a maid doesn't sound like you were telling the truth."

"She was the only one."

"Bullshit."

He really hated me at that moment. Senators don't get pushed around the way regular folks do. Many of the laws that apply to us don't apply to them. And they don't take kindly to regular folk challenging them.

"The truth, Warren. I have to know what might be coming at us sometime. You know, like Clinton's 'bimbo eruptions.'"

He sat back and for a long moment closed his eyes. He wasn't a drama queen, so this kind of behavior told me that he had some serious fessing up to do.

"Six or seven others," he said when he returned to earth.

"In what period of time?"

"The last year, say."

"All one-night stands?"

"All but one. A stewardess. We got together three times."

"All in Washington?"

"No. All here. In Chicago. I have a small apartment absolutely no-body but me knows about."

"You said the last year. How about the last two years? How many would that be?"

"Probably about the same number. Six, seven a year."

"So we're talking twelve to fourteen potential scandals."

"They won't talk. Hell, a few of them are married. They sure aren't going to risk their family life."

"How many are married?"

"What difference does it make?"

"How many?"

"Shit, I don't know. Say, uh, four."

"Four from twelve leaves eight. Eight potential bimbo eruptions."

"They haven't said anything so far."

"So far. But three weeks is a long, long time. And maybe one or two of them are mad because they wanted more than a one-night stand. It's not very often that a woman gets to sleep with a real senator. But you blew her off. So every time she sees your face on TV she gets mad and hurt and vengeful. Most women just ride with it. They don't want to humiliate themselves by getting caught up in a scandal. But there's always one who's like all those people you see on trash TV. 'Sure I'm having sex with my mother, but I'm on TV and that's all that matters.' Maybe one of these eight women you feel so confident about, Warren—maybe at this very moment she's picking up the phone and calling Lake headquarters and saying that she's got a piece of information that's so hot she'll only talk to Lake himself. Remember Paula Jones, Warren?"

"You're scaring the hell out of me, Dev. And I mean that."

"Well, you're scaring the hell out of me, too. Right now I want to punch your face in."

"I don't blame you."

"Oh, don't cheese this up with remorse, Warren. You lied to me and now we're all in trouble."

"Well, excuse me for saying I'm sorry. I guess that's a no-no with big bad Dev, huh?"

"We've got Greaves—or rather he's got us—and we've got to explain to the press about last night, and we've got a campaign to run. If we've got time to squeeze it in between everything else, that is. And then on top of it all we've got maybe one or two women who just might like to see you take a real hard fall."

By this time he was pale and sweaty and a familiar tic had started working on his left eye. The tic usually appeared when stress reached overload proportions for him. He was suffering and I was happy to see it. He'd lied to his wife, to his staff, and to me. Laura had told me soon after I'd signed on that he'd gathered them all together one day and told them in a very formal way, "I am changing my lifestyle. I want to become an adult instead of this compulsive teenager I've been all my life." He didn't have to elaborate. He didn't have to say that heretofore he couldn't seem to keep it in his pants. They knew what he was talking about.

"So now what, Dev?"

"Now we just go on and do our jobs and hope for the best. I want to see Greaves's video, and then I want to see if I can find that makeup woman."

"She doesn't matter anymore."

"Sure she does. If she'll admit that Greaves or somebody else from the Lake camp hired her, we can coast the rest of the way home. We'll wind up with a ten-point lead."

"But what about the tape?"

"Separate issue. I'll look at it and tell you if I think it's been altered in any way."

"But I'll never be able to come up with a million dollars."

"You won't have to. Get me three hundred thousand in cash. I'll bring that to him when we make the swap. He'll piss and moan, but the sight of all that green—he'll come around."

"God, I hope you're right."

"Yeah," I said, "I hope I'm right, too."

CHAPTER 10

Daily Double Discount was located in what had once been a two-story concrete block building belonging to the YMCA. The neighborhood had gotten too rough for the Y folks, so they'd sought safer digs.

The interior had the eternal smell of Salvation Army and Goodwill stores, that faint whiff of the grave that is actually an amalgam of fabrics, mustiness, and the inexplicable scent of decay.

The merchandise was thrown on long folding tables and displayed as was. No racks, no hangers, not even any signs directing you to clothes, housewares, appliances, and so on. I assumed the second floor was more of the same. I browsed the shirts while I waited for the two women up front wearing matching DDD blouses to finish talking to a customer.

Every shirt I picked up had some small thing wrong with it. A pocket had been stitched wrong. One sleeve was a few inches shorter than the other. Color was faded here and there. These kinds of factory rejects could be bought for a fraction of regular wholesale price and sold cheap. I wandered back to housewares and found that all the boxes the irons and mixers and lamps came in were pretty badly banged up. Some of the boxes were crushed, some were so worn on the edges that only the cardboard base was left. Presumably the appliances worked.

A Christian radio station filled the tinny speakers stationed on walls throughout the store. It used to be said that the devil got all the good music. These days it was the reverse. Christian music could claim lots of stars who were talented musicians and singers. My problem was the lyrics. I'd once heard a song where a young woman sang to Jesus as if he were her lover. It made me very uncomfortable. *Hey, Jesus, let's get it on, dude.*

The people were heartbreaking to watch. No matter how low the prices were, they were still too much for many of the customers, those being members of America's first official underclass—black, white, brown, red, physically challenged, mentally challenged, druggies, winos, the perpetually underemployed, people so old they didn't have to die to become ghosts, people possessed of rashes, scars, boils, walleyes, black teeth, yellow teeth, no teeth, the crippled, the insane, the grotesquely fat, the junkie thin—all these being things that a good job with a good health plan could cope with if not resolve, except for the junkies and the insane. Many of these minds would be focused on survival basics—what kind of grub they could scrounge up for dinner tonight. And the place was packed with them.

I went back up front. The black woman at the register said, "Help you, sir?"

"I hope so."

She had a sweet smile. "Well, I'll try, anyway."

The first thing I did was give her the physical description of the makeup woman. I didn't bother giving her the name, because the name was a phony. "She might be or have been a hairdresser who knew something about makeup. For TV. A lot of local newspeople get makeup advice when they get their hair cut."

She had a button with a photo of her granddaughter on it. Cute little two- or three-year-old. She touched it as she squinted her eyes, furrowed her brow, trying to shape all the words I'd given her into a picture.

She didn't address me. She called another cashier over. "Nikki, this gentleman is trying to find a woman he thinks may come in here. I can't place her, but you work nights half the time. Maybe she comes in then."

Nikki was white, thirty-something going on sixteen what with the nose ring, the tongue stud, the goth eye makeup, the spiky bottle-blond hair. If her face was hard, her body was soft in an extremely pleasing way.

She started shaking her head before I got halfway through my description. "That could be several of our customers. Is there anything weird about her?"

"Weird?"

"Yeah, you know. Like a sloe eye or big nose or a scar or something?"

"Not really."

"Hmm." Then, "You know who might know her? Janine in back. She's tried just about every hair place in the neighborhood. She's very, very picky. She probably knows everybody who works around here."

"Could I talk to her?"

"Sure. C'mon, I'll take you back."

"Thank you," I said to the black woman.

Janine was indeed a fan of hair salons. She had a cast-iron hairdo that had last been seen in the known universe around 1960, a kind of modified reddish hair helmet that was a perfect complement to the wild makeup that gave her the look of a sinister doll. I put her age at fifty-five or so.

Nikki did the introductions and left me alone with Janine, whose job, apparently, was going through the warehouse part of the store and matching the numbers on her clipboard with the numbers on the boxes stacked from floor to ceiling. They'd damned well better tally.

"Makeup, huh? Those are the hardest ones to find. Just because a gal knows hair don't mean she knows squat about makeup. And I've tried 'em all. And you know what? I do my own makeup now. I used to tell them how I wanted it to look—just the way it is now—and they'd try and talk me out of it. Every single time. Hey, who knows what I want better than I do? That's what I finally decided, anyway."

"So nobody comes to mind?"

"Sort of—vaguely, I mean. I mean, there was somebody who was supposed to be a real pro with makeup—and I'm sure I tried her, too—but right now I can't get a name or a face. You got a phone?"

"Why don't I give you my cell phone number?"

"You ever read those things can give you brain cancer?"

"I've read that. Some studies say yes, some studies say no."

I wrote my number out and handed it to her.

"If I come up with anybody, I'll call you."

"I'd really appreciate it."

She patted her hair helmet. "I just wish my hair gal knew about makeup. If I had the time, I'd sit her down and explain it to her."

She was deranged but oddly likable. But then I realized that this description could probably apply to me, too. "I'm sure she'd appreciate that," I said and got out of there.

A breast, a thigh, a buttock, a young woman easing herself down on a man's penis. Breath coming in bursts, gasps. She has a fine, tight, lithe body. A couple very clear shots of her face. Surprisingly pretty.

The man—our own Senator Warren Nichols—is also seen very clearly at least three times in the eight-minute videotape. He looks a lot better with his clothes on. He is also less than an ardent lover. He just wants to get off. He could be having sex with an inflatable woman. He just keeps wrenching her into whatever position is best for him at any given moment. A few of the positions are obviously painful for her and she mutters protests. Not that he gives a damn. Not that he tries to be any more considerate. Not that he treats her like any kind of equal.

His cry is almost savage when he comes. Her expression is almost comic in the disgust and contempt it conveys as she watches him fall off her, sated and out of breath, flinging his arms out and lying on his back.

"You're quite the lover."

But he doesn't catch the sarcasm. Through gasps, he says, "Thank you. You're not bad yourself."

If he notices her slipping from the bed, tugging on her thong, combing her hair with her fingers, you can't tell it from what the camera eye sees. He still seems to be riding the wave of his orgasm.

"See you," she says, a slight figure moving swiftly to the door.

"You take care of yourself now," Warren says from the bed.

R. D. Greaves's laugh was harsh. "Your man is some lover. Shit, I've treated whores better than that. Even the ones that gave me crabs."

His hotel room apartment was a nice one. Too nice for somebody like good old R.D. There were two Renoir prints, a massive TV, and a screened fireplace with an imposing natural stone hearth with rough edges. I would have been even more appreciative of the living room if I hadn't been brooding over the videotape.

"So, Sport, now you know I'm not bullshitting you, right?"

We sat in chairs side by side in front of the TV set. Curtains drawn. Day for night.

"I guess."

"You guess my ass. This is the real thing and you know it."

"A million dollars—we can't come up with it."

"Listen, man, I had my accountant check him out. That much cash is always a hassle, but it's there to be had. And if I don't get it by tomorrow noon—"

"I get sick of your threats."

"Well, I get sick of your bullshit."

"How about opening the drapes?"

"Scared of the dark?"

The sunlight was so stark it made me wince. This was one of those Midwestern turnaround days that would be unimaginable anywhere else. A near blizzard last night. Forty-two degrees this morning, the snow melting so fast it was flooding certain parts of the city.

I was thinking about tomorrow, about what I had planned for it when I came back to this room just before noon. It was crude but it would work. It had damned well *better* work, anyway.

"So what's it going to be?"

"We don't have much choice, do we? Tomorrow noon, you'll have your money. Where do I bring it?"

"Right here."

"There's no point in asking you if this is the only copy. I'm sure you've made several dupes of it. And I'm also sure you're going to come back for more."

"Not unless I blow through that million awful fast."

"That's reassuring."

"I don't get the full million tomorrow, asshole, I'm going to feed you to the rats. I don't like people who waste my time."

I walked over and picked up my coat and slid my arms into it. "What happens if Lake ever finds out that you didn't turn the tape over to him?"

"What happens? Nothing happens, because he'll never find out. You sure as hell won't tell him, because then he'll know your secret. And I sure as hell won't tell him, because then he'd tell everybody what I did, and that wouldn't exactly be good for my business rep, now, would it?"

"Nothing's ever that easy, Greaves. You should know that by now. You've convinced yourself that this is the easiest money you've ever made. But you know how things can happen, things you don't expect at all."

A sneer. "If you're trying to scare me, man, it won't work. I want a million in hundred-dollar bills, just the way I told you. Then I'll worry about the rest."

At the door, I said, "I'm still going to nail your ass for drugging the senator's drink last night."

He smiled. "You never quit, do you?"

"Not when I'm after a scumbag like you."

"Aw, there you go again, Sport. Hurting my feelings. I guess you just don't know how sensitive I am. You get me?"

"Oh, yeah," I said, "I get you all right."

"I didn't have jack to do with putting anything in his drink. And neither did Lake. If he had, I would've known about it. He would've asked me to do it."

The sunlight highlighted the coarseness of his face. The old pock-marks, the furious redness of the booze over the years. Once again I didn't want to believe him, but I did. Nothing to do with rigging Warren's drink.

"You got some nice pussy working for you. Don't suppose you'd line me up."

"Only way they'd ever go out with you, 'Sport,' is if they could wear biohazard suits."

"You're forgettin' how sensitive I am."

I got out of there without him winking at me. A small victory.

CHAPTER | 11

✵ ✵ ✵ ✵ When I got back to headquarters, I found Teresa Nichols, Kate, Laura, Gabe, and Billy sitting in Warren's office drinking coffee and looking glum. They were like seven-year-olds who'd just been told they couldn't go outside and play in the tornado.

Billy said, "Have you heard the radio in the last five minutes?"

"I just listen to the oldies station. The eighties was my decade. You know, when I was still innocent."

Laura dredged up a smile. "You were never innocent, Dev."

"All right, but I was at least *semi*-innocent."

"That I can live with."

"I'm afraid to ask, but what was on the radio?"

"Oh, Dev," Teresa said. "It was awful."

"Okay, which one of you is going to give me the first clue?"

"They didn't spend much time on Senator Nichols at all," Kate said. "Most of it was about how heroic and manly and family values Jim Lake looked walking across the stage last night to help his opponent."

"They of course mentioned that he led us in prayer?"

"Of course, Dev. They mentioned that twice, in fact."

Billy said, "They even mentioned the American flag he had stuck up his ass. Forgive my crudity, Teresa."

"Be my guest," Teresa said.

"God, can you imagine what the overnight polling is going to look like?" Laura said.

"Where's Warren?" I asked.

Laura said, "I got him another big radio interview."

They were all here. "He's down there alone?"

"I thought I'd leave pretty soon."

"You leave right now," I snapped at Laura. "Dammit, you're communications director, remember? Get going."

"There's no need for that, Dev," Teresa said. "I was planning on going with her. Sometimes you treat my husband like a helpless child."

"No offense, Teresa, but sometimes he *is* a helpless child. He gets overwhelmed and says the wrong thing. That's why he's hired all of us here. To save him."

She decided to let me live. She sighed and said, "I suppose Dev's right, Laura. We'd better get down there."

"It's only ten minutes on the Dan Ryan," Billy said helpfully.

Before the door closed, and spoken so loudly that I couldn't possibly miss it, Laura said, "I see Dev's on the rag again." And Teresa laughed, of course.

"You could have handled that a little better, Bunny," Kate said, standing up and walking over to get her coat from the rack. Bunny was her nickname for me. I'd never understood why exactly.

"I suppose I could have."

"Technically, you were right. I don't know what the hell Laura was thinking. She said she'd meet him at the studio. But I was starting to wonder when she was going to leave. But still—we don't need the stress of you losing your temper."

"You can't see it, but I'm actually groveling, Kate. I'll apologize to Laura first chance I get. And was the radio really that bad?"

"I've monitored five different stations," Billy said. "Every one of them leads with how noble Lake was before they even mention the senator's name. And since the senator is now up and around, the rest of the time is spent on how voters may now take a fresh look at Jim Lake, who the Nichols campaign and a lot of newspapers have tended to turn into a nut job who's in the pocket of every crooked corporation in the United States."

"The poor baby," Kate said as she left.

Gabe, pouring himself some coffee, said, "This too shall pass, Dev."

"I wish I could believe that."

"Look who we're dealing with here," Gabe went on. "The guy who said that any Catholic who votes Democrat should be excommunicated."

"Lake took it back."

"But it shows that he'll self-destruct. He probably would've done it at the debate the other night if somebody hadn't fixed Warren's Diet Pepsi."

"Maybe Gabe's right, Dev. Lake does tend to self-destruct."

"Yeah, Billy, and maybe Warren can fly without needing a plane."

"Lake always ends up saying the wrong thing," Gabe said.

"Will you guarantee that in writing?"

He appreciated the humor. "Sure. If I don't have to sign my real name."

That afternoon, despite being pretty much drained from last night, I played handball for an hour. I was hoping to find a pickup opponent in the gym somewhere in the age range of eighty to ninety or who was legally blind. Unfortunately, the only guy I could find was about twenty-five and looked as if he bench-pressed Buicks to impress his girlfriends.

He did me the favor of reviving me. I forgot everything but the game. If I hadn't paid attention, he would have literally run over me. He saw what we were doing as mortal combat. He was a video-game star come to psychotic life. I don't think he chuckled the word "pussy" more than four or five times when I missed plays. I was about fifteen years and many muscle groups older than he was. Afterward he congratulated me in the manner of an invading general patting the loser on the back. "You gave it your best, man." I wondered how many times I could hit him in the face before he broke me in half. Well, "Pussy" was at least better than "Pops."

After showering, I found a deli that served Heineken and had myself a corned beef sandwich. I was playing hooky and I knew it. But finally the work ethic snuck up on me and dragged me back to headquarters. The press was gone. Phones, faxes, copiers, deliveries, minor crises—we were back to serious work again. And people of all ages, colors, religions, and degrees of power dreams ran about the place like the Japanese in those old Mothra monster movies cable can buy for cheap on Halloween.

"I think you need a cup of coffee," I said when I walked into the office in the back. Warren was alone, staring off with a frown making him look older than he was.

"I need a lot more than that, Dev. Friend of mine says the *Trib* is going to run a big piece on Jim Lake tomorrow. Family, friends, the whole nine yards. He's our new hero." He snorted and shook his head. "Let us now all bow our heads and pray. Shit, if I'da known it was that simple I woulda brought some holy water along and blessed everybody in the audience. I was an altar boy, you know—and, no, I didn't get buggered by a priest. You can't say you were an altar boy anymore without somebody asking if some priest slipped you the sausage."

"Elegantly put. Now, c'mon. We're going down the street for coffee."

When the waitress brought us our Danish along with our coffee, Warren said, "So you saw the video?"

"I saw the video." We had to speak much more softly this afternoon. The place was only half full. Words carried.

"It's legit?"

I nodded. "I'm done the day after the election."

I took some pleasure in his startled reaction. "What the hell's this all about?"

"Just what I said it was about. I'm quitting the day after the election. Win or lose."

"I see. You're getting sanctimonious on me. Thanks a lot. My ass is on the line here and you're leaving."

"Not till it's over."

"This is really bullshit, Dev."

"You lied to me. When I signed on, I said no lies."

"Well, you sleep around as much as I do and—" He stopped. "Before you give me a sermon, Monsignor Dev, let me correct that statement. When you sleep around as much as I *used to*—"

"It's all bullshit, Warren."

"What is?"

"You've never stopped sleeping around. You've just figured out a way to hide it better."

"Here comes the sanctimony."

"The tape is for real. And so is his demand."

"He wants a million in hundred-dollar bills. We're taking him the three hundred thousand. Right?"

"Right."

"What if he wants more?"

"He won't."

"But what if he *does*?"

"Don't worry. I can handle it. As much as I don't want to."

"And here I thought people in Congress were sleazy. This Greaves is something else, isn't he?"

"Both sides have got people like him."

"Oh, I forgot what you always say. That it's a matter of degrees. Well, thank God we don't have anybody as bad as Greaves."

"I need to know when the money will be ready."

"Tomorrow morning. I should be in the office by ten o'clock."

"Fine."

"Just don't do anything crazy, Dev. Sometimes you worry me. You've got a dark side, my friend. You need to watch yourself."

"Do something crazy like sleep around on camera when I'm up for reelection, you mean?"

"I was hungover. I've told you that. Different men react to being hungover in different ways. I always get this incredible hard-on."

"You could always abuse yourself."

"When a little dolly like her walks in? C'mon, not even a pious bastard like you could resist."

"Maybe, maybe not."

"I wish you'd make me feel a little better about all this, Dev. It wouldn't hurt you to tell me this is going to work out all right."

I couldn't help myself. As much as I'd come to despise him, I felt sorry for him for just a millisecond here. "Warren, you're so used to people propping you up, it's sort of humorous. They forgive you everything and when you're down they pump you back up with bullshit. And that goes triple for when you and the rest of them are in session. You people in Washington are the most spoiled, pampered, self-important group anywhere in the world. And it just keeps on getting worse. You vote yourself more and more privileges every term. And that goes for both sides as always. So when you're faced with a serious crisis that you just happened to cause yourself—you just assume that somebody on your staff can make it all better. Well, I'm going to tell you that maybe this will come out all right and maybe it won't."

"But you said—"

"I said I *think* he'll go for the three hundred thousand. But what if he doesn't? I could kill him and take the tape. You want me to kill him for you, Warren?"

"C'mon. That's crazy. That's what I meant about your dark side."

I leaned back in the booth. Stared right at him. "You love your Senate seat so much, Warren, that if it came right down to it—if the only way you could keep it was to have me kill Greaves for you—"

"Don't be ridiculous."

"I'm not being ridiculous. Maybe in the end you wouldn't be able to give me the order to off him. But I'll bet you'd have to think about it for a long time. And there're a lot of others in Congress just like you. It's just unthinkable that you'd give up power, isn't it?"

"I don't like you anymore, Dev. I really don't."

"Right now," I said, sliding out of the booth, "I could give a shit, Warren."

CHAPTER 12

Dinner that night was a rare delicacy known as a cheese-and-onion pizza that Laura and I shared as we discussed our next media buy. An internal poll had come in late this afternoon that I was seeing for the first time at headquarters. Our interpretation of it was that we were losing whatever gains we'd made downstate, which is more conservative than most people realize. We'd never planned on winning that area of the state, but we had to get a minimum of twenty percent of it to offset any sudden surge by Lake. One of our own pollsters faxed us an internal poll he'd conducted late yesterday. It showed that downstate we were running sixteen percent, down three since Lake had started playing Doc Savage. We'd been at twenty-one a week ago.

"I'd say it's time to unload number four on them. The nuke."

I'd said this with an air of bravado as a joke. Laura had been anxious to drop the most negative commercial we'd ever done. The one that pointed out that if you were an average citizen, it didn't make any sense to vote for Lake.

But she didn't return my smile. Her brown eyes were fixed on a spot slightly to the right of me. She was gazing off into the middle distance, distracted by something that had been bothering her even before I'd walked in here twenty minutes earlier.

"The nuke, Laura. The one you've been waiting for."

"Oh, that'll be great," she said, forcing her attention back to me. The delicate bones of her face were as refined as ever. But in the eyes and in the voice there was a hint of agitation she was having a hard time controlling. "The big one."

"We've got plenty of money. We can saturate the whole area. We can force him to answer us point for point."

But she was staring off again. The temptation was to say something to her, but I decided to turn around and work on the computer for a while.

I called up the copy for the nuke spot. It was simple, and every charge it made was true. Each accusation was based on Lake's voting record.

Ask Jim Lake why he voted against
HEALTH CARE (for those who can't afford it)
EXTENDED UNEMPLOYMENT INSURANCE
TAX PENALTIES FOR COMPANIES OFFSHORE
STUDENT LOAN INTEREST REFORM
CAPS ON LOBBYIST SPENDING
MORE CONGRESSIONAL OVERSIGHT ON GOVERNMENT SPENDING
Ask Jim Lake. You won't believe what he's got to say.

Negative advertising has a bad name. A good deal of it is deceitful and excessive. But used properly, it's the best way to give the public an indication of what your opponent truly believes. This spot was aimed, as most negative ads are, at independent voters who might have started leaning toward Lake. We hoped we were raising at least one issue that would give each voter pause. A saturation campaign was our best hope of achieving that.

A t first I didn't want to believe what I was hearing. The campaign was getting difficult enough. But when it didn't stop, I had no choice except to admit what I was hearing and then turn around and face it.

Laura, dutiful Laura, always reliable communications director Laura, was holding a Kleenex up to her eyes dabbing the tears gleaming down her cheeks. Her nose was red. The hand that held the tissue was trembling.

"Can I help, Laura?"

She shook her head and started crying again, snuffling into the Kleenex. I shoved the box of tissues closer to her. "Probably time to change that one, Laura."

She laughed raggedly, pitched the used tissue into the wastebasket, and then plucked a fresh one from the box.

"You don't think it'd help to talk about it?"

She shook her head again.

"Somebody sick in your family? Something like that?"

"I really can't talk about it, Dev," she managed to say.

"There's a bottle of bourbon in that desk over there. Would you like a shot of it?"

Another shake of the head.

And then she was on her feet, gathering up her coat and purse, clutching them to her as if she were afraid I'd take them away from her. "I just don't know how much longer I can do this," she said.

What the hell was "this"?

"You mean this job? Is that what you're saying, Laura?"

"I'm sorry, Dev. I really have to go. I wouldn't be able to concentrate tonight, anyway. I'll be here bright and early in the morning. I promise. But now—"

She stumbled as she walked to the door. I was afraid she was going to fall over. But she righted herself at the last moment. "I always told you I was a clumsy oaf."

"And I always told you you were crazy."

"I'm sorry to do this to you, Dev."

"Well, you're obviously in no shape to work, so don't worry about it. I just wish you'd let me help you with it, whatever it is."

"Sometimes you can be so sweet, Dev. We all appreciate it."

And then she was just footsteps heard out front in the public section of headquarters. She took the side door out so she wouldn't have to face the volunteers who'd been working late as the campaign hurried to Election Day.

Not a clue. "I don't know if I can do this much longer, Dev." Buy media? Sit in the same room with me? Associate with political people? Face an unhappy life every morning when she got up?

I wasn't worried about her as an employee. She was damned good, but so were others we could sign on quickly. I was worried about her as a friend. I'd never thought of her as being especially vulnerable. She liked to be tough to the point that it was sometimes comical. To see her break this way was shocking.

F luffy scrambled eggs, warm toast with peach jam, two strips of crisp bacon, and a cup of rich, good coffee. Breakfast next morning.

I'd spent a half hour in the hotel gym. I needed to be as focused as possible for my confrontation with Greaves. He'd find out too late that

I'd tape-recorded everything he'd said to me during our upcoming exchange at noon. Then I'd have a bartering tool as well. He might be able to sink the campaign with his video of Warren, but I'd be able to put him in prison for several years for extortion.

He'd come at me, of course, and I wanted to be sure I could take him out fast and sure. I even spent twenty minutes on the punching bag.

Now, after a shower and a change of clothes, I was enjoying my breakfast. Enjoying it right up to the point where one of the city's more prominent Lake supporters suggested in an op-ed piece that officials had conspired to cover up Warren's real problem at the debate the other night, that he'd been drunk.

The op-ed went on to remind voters that not that long ago there were many rumors about Warren in Washington. His girl chasing was one, but so was his excessive drinking.

Had police and hospital officials floated the "sedative" story to cover up his drinking? Nichols was, it went on, a powerful sitting senator and had enough influence to ask them to cover for him.

The charge was ridiculous—maybe you could get cops to cover up a story; hospital officials would never go along with it—but it sounded more convincing than our true story of something being put in his Diet Pepsi and vague hints of a conspiracy.

The lynch mob that listened to talk radio would be sexually excited by an allegation like this. By midafternoon they'd have painted Warren not only as a drunken philanderer but as a terrorist spy as well.

"I want to know what you and my husband are keeping from me."

I raised my head from the op-ed page, happy that somebody had distracted me, and saw a familiar and alluring face across the booth from me. Teresa Nichols was wearing a red ski sweater, her lustrous blond hair pulled back in a pert ponytail. Only the anxiety in her gleaming eyes spoiled the magazine-ad glamour of her patrician face.

"And good morning to you, Teresa."

She smiled. "I'm sorry. I should at least have said hello, shouldn't I? It's just I know he's hiding something. And since he doesn't have any secrets from you—"

"I'm not sure that's true, Teresa."

She had coffee only. Black. When we were alone, the hotel coffee shop starting to fill up with the last rush of the morning, she said, "He's been so distracted the last few days, it's like he isn't even there. And last night I was sure something was wrong."

"What happened last night?"

"Nightmares. He never has nightmares unless something terrible is wrong. He woke up twice shouting and covered in sweat."

"A lot of things could cause nightmares. It doesn't have to be a deep dark secret."

"How about a three A.M. phone call?"

"Now you might be on to something. Any idea who called?"

"No. It came on his cell. He grabbed it and took it down the hall in the den so I couldn't hear it."

"You didn't hear any of it?"

"He muttered a curse word when he answered it in our bedroom. I didn't hear any of the rest of it."

Now she had me curious, too. There was the possibility that the phone call had nothing to do with Greaves and his videotape. But three A.M.—it was difficult to believe that the call wasn't about the tape. There were always sudden campaign problems. But a three A.M. call made it unlikely that an aide had phoned him. He or she would have waited till morning.

"He said you're going to get together about ten at headquarters."

"That's the plan."

"Please do me a favor and see what you can find out. Tell him you had breakfast with me and that I was very concerned."

She still had a good wife's faith that her husband would tell the truth to a close friend and thus, eventually, to her. But Warren was a man of a thousand secrets. I knew only a few of them. I was assuming that this was about the tape. But possibly there was another secret I knew nothing about, something even more dire than R. D. Greaves's tape.

"I'll see what I can do."

She settled back into the booth, a shiny, fine, middle-aged woman I'd had innumerable fantasies about over the years. She was just so damned *clean* and sleek.

"I see you're reading that stupid op-ed."

"The one where he's an opium smoker and a pedophile?"

"I wish it *was* funny, Dev. But I know a certain percentage of people will believe it. He really has changed, Dev. No more chasing around. I'm sure of that."

"Truth doesn't matter to these people, Teresa." And it doesn't matter all that much to your husband, either.

"God knows Warren isn't perfect. But nobody is. For all his faults he's been a very good senator."

"Yes, he has."

"And I still think Jim Lake was behind putting something in his soda the other night."

"Maybe so."

She made a fist with her tiny hand. "Oh, this op-ed just makes me so mad, Dev."

She left the booth as quickly as she'd appeared in it. "I'm meeting Kate for coffee at Starbucks down the street. She's taking her morning break in about ten minutes."

Mention of Kate made me think of another staffer, Laura. And her strange breakdown last night. Another secret I didn't know anything about? What had upset her so much that she couldn't stop herself from breaking down in front of me?

"Nice that you and Kate get along so well."

"God, people keep saying that. I guess they expect a catfight or something. But Kate's been working with us for six years now. We've always been good friends." She glanced at the slender gold watch on her left wrist. "Need to go, Dev. But please try and find out what's bothering him so much, will you?"

"I sure will, Teresa. You just relax and have a good time with Kate."

She leaned over and kissed me on the cheek, the touch of her lips and her perfume arousing me instantly.

I had more coffee and tried not to look at the op-ed page again. But of course I did. Maybe I could get the full-mooner who'd written this in a death cage match. We'd raise money for charity and I'd get to kill him legally.

I was about to leave the booth myself when I looked up from my newspaper and saw a familiar dark face. Detective Sayers.

He slid in across from me. "Sun's out. Glad to see it. You look tired, by the way."

"I wouldn't know why. I'm just rereading the op-ed that says my client is a sleazy bum."

Sayers brushed his chin with a large hand. "And that's not the only problem you have."

I didn't say anything until after he'd ordered coffee and a bagel for himself. "So you brought me more bad news?"

"Not 'brought you.' You already had it. You're too smart not to have figured it out."

"I'm not sure what we're talking about here."

"We're talking about your man passing out onstage the other night. We're talking about who put the stuff in his drink. And we're talking about it probably being an inside job."

"Meaning?"

"Meaning somebody on your own staff."

I settled back. Whatever energy I'd managed to scrounge up at the gym was waning now. The weariness was back. Not only somebody on our own staff—what about the makeup woman?

"There were a lot of people backstage from four-thirty on. We canvassed everybody. Nobody reported seeing anybody who didn't belong there."

He hadn't taken off his tan Burberry. His brown fedora sat on the edge of the table. "I'd like you to be my point man on the inside."

"I believe that's called 'ratting people out.'"

"TV talk. You need to know who you're dealing with and so do I. We want the same thing. The bad guy."

I couldn't disagree. Whoever had given Warren the drug deserved to be identified and punished. "I'm not going to name any names until I'm positive."

"Fair enough. I've got three other cases I'm working on. I'll let you figure out who we're talking about here and then I'll take over when it's appropriate."

"This won't be fun."

"You're friends with all of them?"

"We don't hang out together. Not that type of friends. But when you work as closely with people as I do—you want to see them happy. And succeed. You don't like to think of them as some kind of twisted nut jobs."

He smiled with big white teeth. "You should have my job. You get used to twisted nut jobs real fast."

Somebody at headquarters had blown up the op-ed piece to five times its normal size and made obscene comments in the margins. This would have to come down before a visiting reporter saw it. In the old days, Kennedy's babes and Nixon's innumerable lapses into insanity would never have been reported. (Thanks to Dr. Henry Strangelove Kissinger, we knew that Nixon prayed in his final days in office and urged Strangelove to do likewise; but why would Strangelove pray—when he was God himself?)

When I walked into the office and closed the door, Warren was swallowing two pills from a small brown prescription bottle. Because we were pros we'd moved past our bitter exchange yesterday. Nothing more needed to be said.

"Xanax."

"I thought they made you a little fuzzy."

"Maybe I need to be a little fuzzy."

"According to the schedule you've got four different stops today."

"Maybe you'd rather I come apart when I'm speaking to people."

"Pull a Jimmy Swaggart. There's still time to train that lower lip of yours to quiver the way his did. And then you can start sobbing and go into 'I have sinned.' "

He fixed me with an angry stare. He was lousy at self-pity, as most arrogant people are. "You don't give a shit about me personally, do you, Dev?"

I'd been wrong. He was back in his self-pity mode and seemed to have forgotten every single angry word I'd laid on him. He had the enviable ability of forgetting anything too painful to remember.

I gave him the short version. "I give a shit about what you believe politically. You want to accomplish the same things legislatively that I do. In your own patrician way you give a shit about the masses. And so do I, being one of them. But you personally? You told me a lot of lies to get me on board this time, the biggest one being that you were leaving the women alone. And that may not be all of it. I just had coffee with Teresa. She thinks you're hiding some other deep dark secret."

"Oh, God, she's been on my case since she got here the night of the debate. She's so fucking paranoid."

"Gosh, I wonder why."

"You a marriage counselor now, are you, Dev? That'd be funny for a guy who hasn't had anything but one-night stands for three years."

"I guess I'm being sanctimonious again, huh?"

"You want to know who called at three A.M.? It was Greaves. He just wanted to make sure I'd be ready with the money. Sweet, huh? Three A.M."

"I'm sorry that happened to you, Warren. But we both know he's a creep."

I went over and got some coffee.

"You read that op-ed piece?"

"Yeah."

"Damage?"

"You're doing the radio interview in two hours. Dispute every point in the op-ed. Put it right up his ass."

"This is raw meat for those talk-radio bastards."

"Nothing new there. They already hated you. What I want to see is how much mileage Lake gets from the mainstream press. That's what we have to watch out for."

Once I was seated, he went over and got coffee for himself. He was careful about how he talked now. "I had this place swept again at seven this morning, but I'm still nervous about talking."

"Don't blame you."

He nodded to a brown leather valise on the table with the fax. He gave me a thumbs-up. Three hundred K.

"I'm still a little worried about afterward, Dev."

"So am I." I changed the subject quickly. In case the room was still bugged, I didn't want to say anything incriminating. "Laura's having some personal problems."

He seemed surprised. "That's very interesting, but what the hell does it have to do with anything this morning?"

It wasn't the sort of thing I'd usually discuss on the morning I was going to drop off better than a quarter million dollars in cash to a blackmailer, but at least it got us talking about something other than the brown valise and the possibility that Greaves was going to keep on blackmailing us. I'd already ingested half a roll of Tums.

"Thought I'd mention it. I don't see her around this morning."

"She's under a lot of stress. She's a good woman. She'll pull out if it, Dev. And now can we talk about something else? Did anything good happen for our campaign today?"

But I wasn't up for making him feel better. Screw him.

"You go over your notes for the radio interview?"

"Three times. This Mindy Thomas, she's friendly to us, right?"

"She was last time around. Hard to believe she'd go for Lake, though she didn't go for our governor candidate last time."

"He was about as appealing as diarrhea."

"Be sure and mention that on the air."

He laughed. "I can't help it. Even when I'm pissed at you, I laugh at your stupid sarcasm."

"Oh, I forgot. You want to be universally loved."

"Am I that bad?"

"How many times have you studied yourself in the mirror today?" His Washington staffers told me he kept a mirror the size of a hard-back book in his office drawer. Every major politician is a megalomaniac. There are no exceptions, not even the ones who look like parrots and advocate executing abortion doctors. Maybe they are megalomaniacs in particular. But so are the warm and fuzzy ones that everybody likes because they're for "the little guy," a bit of praise that stretches back to at least FDR, who saw just about everybody in America as his personal servant.

"Guess I'll go to the john," he said abruptly. He picked up the new *Time*. "Are we in here this week?"

"Yeah, you're on the cover and half the magazine is your biography."

"Someday that'll be the truth, Dev. You wait and see."

"You'll have to share it with Genghis Khan."

"I'm a lot better looking than he was," Warren said, trundling off.

CHAPTER 13

Laura got in around ten-thirty. I had the valise with the money pushed under my desk. I was trying to concentrate on a couple of niche print ads—one to labor; one to suburban women—that needed to be FedExed by late this afternoon. Either the copy was perfecto or I was so distracted I couldn't read English. I signed my name and initials in big looping letters. I even put an exclamation point on them, making the copywriters' day.

She didn't say anything. Despite the swank blue dress and the swank moussed hair, the dark circles under her eyes and the heavy, anxious sighs betrayed her agitation and sorrow. Sort of like me in the first months following my divorce.

I spoke first. "Mind if I ask how you're doing?"

"How the fuck you think I'm doing?"

"I guess that kind of answers it."

She sat at her desk, sipping coffee and checking her e-mails. I took a couple of inconsequential phone calls.

When I hung up, she said, "I shouldn't have said that."

"Can I be patronizing and say that I've hung from that cross you're on now?"

"Your divorce?"

"Yeah."

"I thought I was tougher than this."

"We all think we're tougher than this. Even professional wrestlers think they're tougher than this."

She giggled. "That was exactly the right thing to say. You are so weird sometimes, Dev, and it's almost always funny."

"I never told you I was a professional wrestler?"

"Billy used to brag about how you were a college boxer. And you were in the army, too?"

"Yeah. Did he add that I got my nose broken twice and had to be taken to the hospital once with a concussion?"

"Nah. He didn't tell me that. Makes a better story without it."

Then she took a deep breath and sighed it out. "For about forty-two seconds there you had me in a good mood. I think that's my record for the last twenty-four hours."

"I went as long as fifty-two seconds in the first month after I got dumped."

"Now I have a goal to shoot for. And please don't tell me that I'm going to feel better real, real, *real* soon. The next fucking person who says that to me is going to get their car blown up."

"I always figured you for a terrorist."

"Didn't you hate all the advice people gave you?"

"I wore those earplugs they wear on aircraft carriers." And I damned near had, too. Admit that you've got a broken heart and suddenly everybody you know turns into a grief counselor. I'm not even sure they mean well. It's a power position, and any number of them, it seemed to me, enjoyed being condescending.

"Tell me to focus."

"Focus, Laura."

"I've got so much to do."

"Focus or I'll beat the crap out of you. I was a boxer, remember."

"Yeah, but you got your nose broken twice."

"And don't forget the concussion. But I could still whip you."

"That did it. You scared me straight. Now I'm one hundred percent concentration."

"Good. So now you'll shut up so *I* can concentrate."

"You sure put in long days," Laura said.

"The burdens of a role model."

"I'm going to the little girls' room and cry my eyes out."

"Really?"

"Really."

"Take plenty of Kleenex."

"Won't need it. Plenty of toilet paper there."

"Ah."

"I actually thought of calling you in the middle of the night."

"You know, I still don't know exactly what you're talking about here."

"Someday I'll be able to tell you."

"Call me anytime you want to, Laura. You know that."

She put her hand in mine. "I really did think I was tougher than this."

"Read Hemingway. He knew we were all cowards in all respects."

"Maybe I'll give him a try."

I was just settling in with my computer when Billy came into the office. "Good morning." He probably wasn't going to feel that way when I gave him some bad news. Billy hated to travel.

"We're having problems in Galesburg," I said. "Our man there had a heart attack, as you know. That was four days ago. In the interim the place has gone totally to shit. I need you to fly there and see if you can get things straightened out. You can be back on a late plane. We already bought you your ticket. You leave in two hours."

"Aw, shit, Dev. I've got things going on here."

"I'm sorry, Billy. You're good at this and you know it. All you have to do is figure out a new organizational chart. The woman who's number two is afraid to make any changes. You know, she'll hurt people's feelings and all that. So you be the bad guy for her."

"Hell, I could do that over the phone."

"Yeah, I suppose you could. But I'd rather you go there personally. Make it a little more official."

"Shit."

"I think you said that already."

The sun had turned Chicago into its usual road race. The streets were reasonably clear, tires could get traction, everybody was late or thought they were, and ordinarily calm, respectable drivers had suddenly begun trying out for the Daytona 500.

And what was Chicago without its sirens? Police, ambulance, firefighters. All day, all night in some sections of the city. By the time I reached Greaves's hotel, I'd been slowed down by two fire trucks and an ambulance.

I knew this was the beginning of Greaves feeding off Warren. Right now I didn't care. Even if we got a monthlong respite from his greediness, it would be enough to work our way back up in the polls and have a good chance of winning by two or three points. It might not be the win we'd hoped for. But it would be a win. And while I didn't have much respect for him as a man, Warren and I did share the same view of what had to be done in this grotesquely unjust society the rich and shameless had turned it into since the early 1980s—Bush, Clinton, Bush—time for a serious new start. The only time I'd felt any support for Clinton after the first term was when the other side had tried to impeach him, talk radio's wet dream. I'd be afraid to impeach just about anybody. Once that door is opened, we'll become Italy within ten years, insurrections a monthly occurrence in the legislature.

The new siren wasn't any different from the ones I'd just passed. Not until I got within two blocks of Greaves's hotel did I see that his block had been cordoned off with yellow crime scene tape and that an ambulance and two police cars were standing in front of the hotel itself.

I knew then. I could have been wrong, of course. But I didn't think so. A man like Greaves lives the kind of life that was once said of the animal kingdom—short, nasty, and brutish.

I wish I could say something noble here. For whom the bell tolls and all that sort of bullshit. But Greaves was a predator, and we've got far too many of them in our society.

I found a parking spot a block and a half away and walked over to the crime scene. I've gotten to know a number of cops over the years. We've hired some of them to supply security for our various functions. We pay well. And over the years they become sergeants and then detectives. And we can call on them for information.

I didn't see a single cop I knew in front of the hotel. The first two print reporters were there by now, too. TV couldn't be far behind. "Hey!" one of the onlookers called. "Who says you can go up there?" And the woman he was with complained, "Who does he think he is?"

I was going to tell her I was Clark Kent, but she probably wouldn't know who that was.

I walked up to a uniformed woman and said, "My sister's staying here. I hadn't heard from her in a couple of days and—"

"Nothing to worry about, sir. This was a man."

I moved as close as I could get to the ambulance and still be on the public side of the crime scene tape. They brought him down on a gurney. Fortunately, there was enough wind to pick up the sheet over his face. I got a millisecond glimpse of him. It was Greaves all right.

A headache started over my right eye. Stress. Wouldn't last long. But for the moment it forced me to close my eyes.

My knees are always the first thing to shake when I lose control for a while. I'm not sure why. Maybe it's some kind of memory from my boxing days. My legs were my weakest point. Four, five rounds and they'd start to go on me. That accounted for the concussion that time. I started to fall into him and he did what any boxer would try to do, take my head off. All thanks to my legs. I walked, wobbly, away from the crime scene.

No problem now worrying if Greaves would take the three hundred thousand.

Now we had much bigger problems.

Who had the tape that he was going to sell us?

CHAPTER 14

The smells of corned beef, pizza, burgers with lots of onions—staff and volunteers were eating a late lunch when I got back to headquarters. None of them paid much attention to me. Maybe I didn't look as mean as I thought. I wanted to smash somebody up, exactly who or why I wasn't sure. Maybe I wanted to smash myself up. Maybe I'd mishandled this whole Greaves thing. We never like to think that we ourselves screwed something up, but this time maybe it really was me.

Laura was typing rapidly on her computer. Kate and Teresa judged as Warren held up various neckties for them to inspect. Gabe was reading a reference book that had to weigh fifty pounds.

"Tell him to keep the one he's wearing," Teresa said of Warren's tie.

"These others are god-awful," Kate said.

"This tie gives me bad vibes," Warren said.

"And he makes fun of astrology," Teresa said. "Bad vibes."

Warren knew the significance of me being back here with the valise still in my hand. He was the one who should be Clark Kent now. His eyes could penetrate the leather and tell which it held—the money or the tape.

"You up for a good Italian meatball sandwich?" Warren said to me. I could gauge his anxiety by him suggesting Italian. All the Tums he took a day even for bland food—Italian food meant he was desperate to get out of here. "We can just walk a block over. Won't need any guards or anything." Teresa was adamant about keeping his protection. He hated people hovering. It gets tiresome. You have to watch what you say. Bodyguards sell a lot of material to gossip columns.

"Sounds good. Lots of fat and cholesterol and maybe spill some of that sauce on me. What more could a guy ask for?"

Kate laughed. "When you first came in here, I thought you were in a real bad mood. But now that you're cracking jokes, I know I was wrong."

Fooled them again.

"You've got to talk to the veterans' group in two hours," Laura reminded him.

"We'll be gone thirty, forty minutes at the most. Dev here will see to it that I'm on time."

"How was the radio interview?"

"One of His Majesty's finest hours," Teresa said. "Right, Kate?"

"We were like schoolgirls," she said, sliding her arm around Teresa's shoulder, "actually swooning, he was so good."

"He got through the questions about the debate very well and right up at the top. He spent the rest of the time contrasting his record with Lake's. You could tell the host was impressed. Off the air she said that he was much better on radio than Lake. She said Lake was too strident for radio. That he came over better on TV, where you could see him, and that helped cut down on what he sounds like."

"Too bad it isn't the other way around," Warren said. "TV is where the big numbers are. A lot more people watch TV than listen to radio at any time."

Kate said, "Never try to flatter our senator here. He reacts very badly."

"Thirty or forty minutes or we'll come and get you, right, Kate?"

"Absolutely."

Ten steps from headquarters, Warren said, "Well, did you get it?"

"No, but Greaves did."

"What's that supposed to mean?"

"It means somebody killed him in his hotel room."

He stopped walking. Stood on the sidewalk, paralyzed. All but the eyes that frogged out a bit. "What the hell are you talking about?"

"Just what I said. Now get a grip, Warren. We're out in public, remember?"

"Somebody fucking murdered him?"

"That's right."

"And we don't know who has the tape now?"

"We don't know one way or the other. Given Greaves's background, we can't be sure that this had anything to do with the tape. There were probably several other people who had reasons to kill him."

Once we were seated in the restaurant, speaking in lower voices, and after he'd waved to everybody who recognized him and a few who hadn't, he said, "What the hell are we going to do now? What if Lake has it?"

"I need to find the makeup woman. See what she knows. Maybe she worked with Greaves."

"And how do you plan to do that, for God's sake?"

"I've seen her. I know who I'm looking for, anyway. There's at least a chance that she lives somewhere in the neighborhood I was in."

"Where would you even start?"

"Beauty shops, bars, dry cleaners. Everywhere."

"I don't like this." Petulant.

"Gosh, I'm sorry this is difficult for you, Warren. Myself, I'm having a great time."

"Don't mock me."

"Then quit feeling sorry for yourself."

"And don't give me any 'wages of sin' bullshit."

"That's your trouble, Warren. You think it *is* bullshit. But it isn't. You do something you shouldn't, you always run the risk of getting nailed. It's pretty simple."

"Thank you, Professor." Then: "We have to get that tape."

"I know, Warren. But you're forgetting the other possibility."

"I won't be able to eat anything now anyway. Tell me."

"Maybe the killer couldn't find the tape in Greaves's hotel room."

"So it's still there."

"So it's still there or the police got luckier than the killer and found it."

"The police." He'd spoken sharply. We both looked around to see if anybody was listening. The Italian music—Dean Martin, of course—covered a lot of sins. And we had a lot of sins to cover. "The police? And what would they do with it?"

"Hard to say. I don't know what the protocol is here. Who they turn it over to. Probably the Cook County State's Attorney's Office."

"Then what?"

"Then I don't know. Like I said. But the big thing right now is to find the makeup woman."

"You have her name?"

"Not really. She made it up. But I may be getting a lead from this store I checked with. I'm pretty sure I've got the right neighborhood for her anyway."

Warren visibly relaxed. "I'm glad you're handling this, Dev. Sorry I came unglued there."

"We just have to be careful here, Warren. We could create even more problems for ourselves if we do anything rash."

"Is there any way the police can link us to Greaves?"

"Depends on what he left behind. Did he keep notes? What's on his computer? Did he have an appointment book? The paper trail's going to figure in here. Not just for us but for the killer, too. The luckiest break we could have is if the paper trail leads the police to the right person right away."

We both passed on the wine. Coffee was what we needed.

He finally did eat his sandwich. I was hungry. I would have eaten half of his if he'd decided to leave it.

"You need to clear your head as much as possible now. And to calm down. No more Xanax, though. You need all the energy you can get. You did well on the radio interview. That's got a big metro audience. That'll help. Probably the interview'll get covered by TV and newspapers. So we're starting back the right way. We've still got the edge in the polls. We can build on that. Heroes don't last long. The press'll now be looking for some way to prove he *isn't* a hero. This is the fun part for them. Knocking somebody down they enshrined as nobility. Plus, when people start to think about it, what the hell did he do, anyway? He was courteous at best. He walked across the stage and gave you a little assistance. Most people, man or woman, would do that. So what? We've got his record to shoot down and we're doing it with our ads and with you on the stump. Once we get this tape thing under control—and I'm hoping that that'll be very quickly—we'll be able to relax a little. But for right now you have to do the old Bill Clinton bit of compartmentalizing. You need to look stronger and tougher than ever, Warren. You need to go out there and start talking about the way we've become such an elitist society. That's your strongest theme. And you've got the voting record to back it up."

He smiled. "I take it that was an official political consultant pep talk?"

But I didn't smile in return. "I'm just doing my job, Warren."

CHAPTER 15

✢ ✢ ✢ ✢ I saw a documentary on a political campaign that
✢ ✢ ✢ mentioned everybody, including part-time volun-
✢ ✢ ✢ ✢ teers, but never said anything about the scheduler.
✢ ✢ ✢ ✢ While it may not sound like a difficult job, it is. You
not only have to decide—usually with the campaign manager's
input—where the candidate will be in the next forty-eight to fifty-six
hours, you have to be ready to make abrupt changes if the waters get
dangerous.

Miriam Dobbs is a quiet grandmother who came out of the AFL-
CIO political wing back when Walter Reuther was still running
things. Ike and Jack Kennedy were presidents then, Elvis was in the
army, and a tubby little man named Khrushchev was our country's
main nemesis.

That Miriam was a black woman made her success even more re-
markable. She's the best scheduler I've ever worked with. She pays attention to the news. She senses when one event will have to be bumped

in favor of another. Today she was working out of our office across town, so we did our work by phone.

"I'm assuming we want max audience to show him off. Strong, sturdy, using his sleeve instead of a tissue when he sneezes."

She also makes jokes.

"I kind of like the sleeve thing. Distinguishes him from the rest of the pack."

"I thought he pretty much did that by eating with his hands."

"You may have a point there, Miriam."

After a few more gags, we settled into a review of the substitutes she'd come up with. All of them were excellent. All of them would attract the press. The previous appointments had been small towns reached by private plane. We could reschedule those for later. For now the city was where he needed to be.

"There's also a chance I can get him a good TV interview."

"Wow. How'd you swing that?"

"My son is a news producer."

"Nepotism, eh?"

"That sounds dirty."

"When will we know?"

"I'm hoping by late this afternoon."

"Let me know, will you?"

"Always."

M y last call from the office was to a friend of mine at one of the big political action committees. PACs have an unseemly reputation, but there are PACs and there are PACs. This one was sponsored by a group of wealthy men who also happened to be hunters. While I'm not much for killing innocent animals, these people were at least enlightened enough to understand the connection between the environment and their favorite sport. We needed some extra money not only for downstate TV but for some massive radio buys the last week before the election.

I sweet-talked my contact there, a soft-spoken young woman named Heather whom I'd dated a few times in Washington. She'd decided that since I was still so hung up on my marriage, being with me was "like being with my brother." She probably wasn't far wrong.

"You're sounding a lot better these days, Dev."

"Feeling better."

"Good." She hesitated. "Now I'm the brokenhearted one."

"What's his name? Consider him rubbed out."

"I committed the single girl's ultimate sin."

"Married?"

"Not only married, three kids, too. I really felt like a home wrecker. I kept trying to break it off with him. I really did feel grubby about the whole thing. Finally he broke it off with me. He had the decency to feel guilty about what he was doing to his family. But I still haven't been able to get over him."

"I'm sorry, Heather."

"Well, my luck's bound to change. I'm sure I'll meet a closeted gay guy in the next week or so."

"There you go."

"Or a wanted fugitive. And speaking of wanted—"

"You could be a disc jockey with segues like that."

"—you of course want money."

"Lots of it and fast."

"What the hell happened to your man the other night?"

"Somebody probably dropped a sedative in his drink."

"Most likely one of the ladies he's been seeing on the side all these years."

"You're too cynical."

"You really don't believe he's changed, do you?"

113

"Hope springs eternal."

"So how much are we talking here, Dev?"

So I told her how much we were talking and I thought she might hang up on me. Luckily all she did was laugh and say, "It's a good thing we've got the same ideas politically."

"Yes," I said, "isn't it, though?"

CHAPTER | 16

I was a suburban kid who grabbed every chance possible to get into the city. My main parental warnings fit into two categories: "strangers" and "neighborhoods." They weren't mutually exclusive, but the former could be anywhere and the latter you had to be lured into. I was on such guard against strangers that I didn't even trust police officers. I'd learned from many science fiction movies that even city officials could be aliens in disguise, which, when you think about it, just may be true.

On the days I took the bus in, I didn't see much in the way of neighborhoods. The route was a three-lane nonstop jaunt that wasn't even long enough to make you sleepy, the way bus trips always seemed to make me. Going in on the train, though, you got to see or at least glimpse a variety of neighborhoods. The rough ones always fascinated me. After all the warnings I'd gotten about them, they held a real interest for me. Scary, for sure. But also intriguing. What were the people like there? If I went in, could I get out alive? And—this was at the age of peak romantic notions—would I find my true love there and then carry her off to the land of three-car families and season tickets for all the Illini football and basketball games?

By now, though, my interest in poor neighborhoods had been trumped by reality. Working for various pols over the years, I'd spent many nights walking streets controlled by gangs and watching the sad, weary working poor try to stave off not only hunger but despair as well. They would listen to us but they wouldn't believe us. You can only hold out hope so many times.

And now, just as the sun began to slant downward in the cloudy sky, I was back in a place where most of the cars had taped windows and wired-shut doors and at least one tire that was nearly flat. Businesses had barred windows. The houses weren't much better. Taped windows, sagging doors, frost-staved sidewalks.

I passed three straight blocks of tiny shops so dusty and old they resembled something out of Dickens. Some of them didn't even identify what they had to offer. I counted four astrology readers on my way in. The taverns were narrow, dark except for the neon signage above the doors and just starting to fill up for the night, men from nearby factories entering in small and hearty groups.

Not even spreading dusk hid the wasteland here. Not even the deepest shadows could lie about the conditions of the houses, the stores, the people. I found the address I was looking for, thanks to the woman from Daily Double Discount. She'd given me the name of a Beth Wells. I slid into an open space along the curb, three car lengths down from where the two-story white house with the slanting side steps sat. I waited twenty minutes before I went up. If she came out I planned to follow her.

While I waited, I saw one of those heartbreaks you want to look away from as soon as you see it—an enormous woman in a cheap gray Goodwill coat came up the sidewalk toward my car, her limp so pronounced that she lurched violently to the left every time she stepped down on her right foot. She must have been three hundred pounds plus and even in the waning light her face showed the claw marks of a vicious skin disease. She kept her eyes downcast. Eye contact for her would be deadly. She wouldn't want to see people smirking or making disgusted faces at the sight of her. You try to think of lives like hers and they're incomprehensible. All the pain; life as the alien, the outcast. I wished I still believed in praying. It was all I could think of to offer her.

By this time of day, NPR was doing lighter stuff, which generally didn't interest me. The jazz station I listened to was doing Dixieland, which didn't interest me, either. I took these two omens as my call to action.

I'd brought along my Glock. I wasn't sure why. Security blanket I suppose.

Since the address listed ended in ½, I interpreted that as being the upstairs apartment. The wooden stairs were just beginning to gleam with frost as I made my way up them. I listened for any kind of sound. Nothing, neither downstairs nor up. No lights, either. Maybe Beth Wells wasn't home. I'd decided against calling her in advance. Didn't want to give her the chance to run away.

At the top of the stairs a voice. Then the door opened. I automatically touched the Glock in my overcoat pocket. And then one of those surprises that is so startling your first impression is that you're hallucinating. *This can't possibly be.* But it is.

He saw me now, too. But I already had the Glock pointed right at his chest. "Back inside."

"What the fuck is the gun for?" He couldn't decide whether to be scared or angry. He was a bit of both.

"Back inside, you bastard. I'll be asking the questions. Not you."

"What's wrong, Billy?" a female voice from inside said.

"Shit," Billy said, "I can't believe this."

I marched him back inside. I kept the gun in sight.

The makeup woman said, "Oh God. It's that guy from the other night."

"My boss," Billy said glumly, talking like a ten-year-old who's been caught stealing apples. "This is so totally fucked I can't believe it."

"Turn on a light," I said.

"God, please put that gun away. I had to live like this all my life with my father. He was always pulling guns on somebody."

"Lights," I repeated as I slammed the door shut behind me.

She clicked on a table lamp, bathing a sorry room of secondhand furniture in dusty gold. One of the end tables was missing a leg and supported by a stack of paperbacks. The couch was so swaybacked that a pair of throw pillows had been placed in the middle of it. Otherwise the sitter would sink out of sight forever. The wallpaper was stained grotesquely in the way of an X ray showing large patches of terminal cancer. Welcome home.

"Both of you on the couch."

"Don't I get to talk?" Billy whined.

"No. Now both of you on that couch."

"Or what? You'll kill us?" the Wells woman said. "I'm so damned sick of all you bullies." But she went over and sat on her side of the couch as Billy sat on his. Nobody wanted to sit in the middle.

I took the overstuffed chair with the ripped arm. Stuffing the color of urine climbed out of the tear. I opened my coat, set the Glock on the good arm of the chair, and said, "You talk first, Billy. How do you know this woman and what're you doing here?"

"You're going to fire me for sure."

Sometimes his naïveté gave me a migraine. He seemed to live in this dreamworld where no matter how badly you fucked up, people just slapped you on the back and said, "Just try and do better next time, Billy old salt, old pal, okay?"

"You're already fired."

Even for somebody who was an old master at looking miserable, Billy gave me a peek at a terror I never want to experience for myself. His dreamworld had gone into nova at last.

"She's my friend."

"I'm his lover. He's just afraid to say it. And he doesn't have to tell you anything."

"The way you didn't have to tell us anything when you dropped that sedative into the senator's glass the other night?"

"Oh God. I should've known you'd accuse me of that. As soon as I heard it on the news, I said to Billy they'd try and put that on me." The shy, quiet girl who'd applied Warren's makeup was now street voluble and street tough. "I didn't have a damned thing to do with it and neither did Billy. Or my father, for that matter. And I never stick up for my father. You can ask Billy if you don't believe me."

"Who's this father you keep talking about?" I said.

"I guess I should tell you now, Dev. Her father is R. D. Greaves."

"Oh, man, what the hell is going on here, Billy?"

"It's not as bad as it sounds, Dev. I promise."

Beth Wells rubbed her fingers against her thumb. "Money. That's the only thing we were trying to get. I'm a beautician and I do makeup on the side. Billy helps me get hired for political things. He was just afraid of what you'd say if you knew who my father was, so we used a fake name and Billy pretended not to know me."

"Good old Billy."

"It's the truth, Dev. Neither of us had anything to do with putting anything in Nichols's glass. I swear."

"It's the truth," she said.

"You called Pauline Doyle at the auditorium and set it all up for Beth," I said to Billy.

"I thought it was pretty harmless."

"How long have you two been going out?" I said.

Their gazes met briefly. Billy said, "Since the last election. Her dad approached me back then. He wanted me to spy for him, spy on Warren, I mean. But I wouldn't do it. That's how I met Beth."

What I was thinking about now was the videotape. If my contact with the police had gotten the correct information, no videotape had been found among Greaves's belongings. Did these two know about the tape?

Beth brought me a glass half full of bourbon with ice cubes. I don't know what I expected, but the glass was clean and it came complete with a cocktail napkin. I'd marked her as being as uncivilized as her old man, but it wasn't a good fit. If her story was true, the worst thing she'd done was have Billy get her makeup jobs for politicians.

I could try to be coy or subtle, but I wasn't in the mood. "Your father contacted me about a videotape."

"What videotape?" she said.

"Please. I've had enough of your bullshit. You *know* what videotape."

Long, ragged sigh. "First you accuse me of putting whatever it was in Nichols's drink. And now you're accusing me of knowing something about a videotape."

"R.D. never told us much, Dev. He really didn't. And I mean about anything. He didn't trust us, I guess."

I didn't want to believe him. But I did.

Billy put a hand on her knee to comfort her.

She slid her hand over his. "He didn't trust anybody. He was even like that with my mom. After she died, I didn't want to live there without her. She was my best friend." Bitterness came into her voice. "He was drunk at her funeral. Made an ass of himself."

"But you kept up your relationship anyway?" I said.

"Yeah," she said, sounding both bitter and oddly wistful. "And you know what? If you asked me why, I couldn't tell you. I suppose because he was father and I was daughter and I just followed the script. I just played out the role. Thank God I met Billy."

I was done here. Such a wonderful, sinister lead—and such a pitifully believable explanation.

"I'm going to make a pizza if you'd like to stay," Beth said, and for some reason in that moment I liked her very much. There was something of my daughter in her.

"Thanks, Beth. But I need to get back to the office."

"Everything cool with us, Dev?" Billy said anxiously.

"Next time just tell me you want Beth to do the makeup, Billy. It'll be a whole lot simpler."

Then I was gone.

CHAPTER 17

Gabe was alone in the headquarters office. I could smell the whiskey as soon as I walked in. Out front, the place was packed with well-wishers and volunteers ready for their nightly assignments. Gabe, in his graying ponytail and granny glasses, sat at his desk with his feet up reading *The Rolling Stone Reader*. At least he wasn't doing any online gambling at the moment. The great Marxist who fell for the worst sucker game of all, gambling. Warren had had to loan him money several times. And as far as I knew, Gabe still owed him many thousands of dollars. He hated Warren for not taking more leftist stands. He hated him even more for having to beg him for money to replace what he'd lost online.

"I was just reading about the '68 Democratic Convention here in Chicago," he said after I'd settled in. "You should've been there. The American gestapo's finest hour. Mayor Daley and his goons. Daley called one of the senators on the stage a fucking kike. You couldn't hear him, but you could see him say it. You could actually read his lips. Then he called out his pigs and his police dogs and it was a mess. I got six stitches in my head."

I'd noticed that left-wing people my father's age recalled even the worst moments of the sixties with a certain fondness. It had been, for many of them, as close to utopia as they would come here on Planet Earth. Yes, they'd been beaten, overdosed on drugs, suffered everything from scabies to incurable syphilis, broken bonds with families that had still not healed, and even been sentenced to prison. They'd had heroes as dubious as Timothy Leary, Bobby Seale, Abbie Hoffman, that only they could see the worth of. But even the worst of it all was cloaked in a nostalgia for that time when they—or so they saw themselves—bravely went up against the establishment that had contrived a war in Vietnam, persecuted blacks, let millions of their countrymen starve, and attempted to brainwash us with the Orwellian words of Nixon and Kissinger. For them these days, now approaching senior citizenship after all, there would never be a drug high, an orgasm, a guitar riff, or a speech as spiritually moving as the one they'd heard back in '66 or '68 or even '79. Those were the sacred days.

"Six stitches? Sounds like a lot of fun, Gabe."

"That's the trouble with you kids today. You came out of your momma's crotch with only one thought in mind. You wanted to get rich. No ideals."

"I think you're either overestimating your generation or underestimating mine." I couldn't look at him without wondering if he was still gambling on the sly. Addicted gamblers are like that.

"I'm hoping you all change. Not you personally, Dev. I mean you're like me, an idealist. You know it'll never happen, but you keep on working at it anyway. The other people around us—politics is a gig for them. They think it's exciting."

"It's probably more exciting than working for an ad agency or a brokerage house."

"But that's all it is—exciting. And most of the time it isn't even that. It's just slogging through to sell your candidate. Who'd sell out his country in a minute if he had to."

"I'm glad I dropped by for your nightly inspiration."

His laugh was bitter. "You know what I'm saying is true. Warren only takes the position he does because that's his niche in politics. Remember, he was on the other side all through college. Was even an activist for them. He changed when he couldn't get the nomination for a seat in the state legislature."

Early in his career Warren had had to answer to that charge many times. There was no way short of a religious conversion that you could play the instant turnaround from one side to the other. And not look dishonest. But a scandal in the statehouse had squeaked him into office and he'd done so well in his first term in Springfield that even the press eventually began to see his conversion as real. Saint Paul on the Road to Damascus was frequently cited by way of explanation these days.

I wanted Gabe to shave the beard and cut the hair and quit wearing the crew necks and faded jeans. I wanted him to face the realities of the sixties and not live in the past. But mostly I wanted him to find peace for himself. There was such sadness in those faded blue eyes and in that cigarette-raspy voice these days. He was a wounded animal. For all his self-delusion, there was a saintliness about Gabe.

"I'm sorry, Gabe."

He'd been staring off. Now his eyes fixed on me. "Sorry about what, Dev?"

"Oh, you know. I'm always sanctimonious about something. Now it's the sixties I'm sanctimonious about. Your generation did a lot of good and the country is better for it."

He took his feet down from the desk, sat up straight. "Ah, who gives a shit anyway?" he said, reaching into his drawer for his pint. "You want a hit?"

"No thanks."

"Mind if I have one?"

"Not at all."

"You're a good man, Dev."

"But sanctimonious."

"Yeah," he smiled. "But sanctimonious."

I worked for about forty-five minutes, worked with enough intensity that I didn't quite realize that Gabe had slipped out and Teresa had slipped in, perching herself on the edge of Kate's desk.

When I paused to rub my eyes, she said, "In your own way, you're a good-looking man, Dev."

"I guess that's a compliment."

"It just means you're not conventionally handsome. You know, like my husband." She sighed. "I'm feeling very sorry for him tonight."

"Oh, right. That press association dinner."

"They're really going to lay it on about the debate."

Gabe came in just as she said that. "The cops doing anything about that by the way, Dev?"

"They claim to be." I hadn't mentioned the obvious to any of the staffers, that it was one of them. And now that I'd met Beth and believed her story, that fact was irrefutable. I had no idea what the police theory was at this point and it really didn't matter.

"How about a hug, Gabe?" Teresa said.

He went over and took her in his arms, careful not to pull her off her perch. Teresa was a collector of lost animals and lost souls. She'd long ago taken pity on Gabe, even when some of the midlevel staffers quietly questioned his value to the campaign. One of them had even drawn a business card that read:

GABE COLBY
Resident Hippie

After Gabe sat down, Teresa said, "Did you tell Dev the news?"

"I was going to but he got busy."

"Always the last to know." But there was something about the tone in her voice, a kind of remorse, that I didn't like.

"I got a book contract to edit a textbook about campaign politics over the last fifty years," Gabe said. "There's enough money for me to retire and do it full-time."

"Hey, that's great." But it wasn't great, because I didn't believe it. What the hell was going on here? I watched Teresa's face. She didn't seem happy.

"Who's the publisher, Gabe?"

"Oh, a a new house, Small press. Rivington House is the name."

I was no expert on publishing, but I wondered if a small press, a start-up yet, could afford to pay the kind of money that would let Gabe retire.

"Yeah, I'm really excited about it," he said. "Something I've always wanted to do."

"So this'll be after the election I take it?" I said.

"Sure, Dev. Hell, the press would have all kinds of questions if I quit now."

Good old Gabe. Maybe he'd finally paid Warren off. Or maybe they were so sick of each other that Warren had agreed to forget the debt and just send him away.

Teresa went over to him and gave him another hug. "Warren and I are really going to miss you." So she didn't know. One thing this staff did was keep things from her. As they many times, apparently, kept things from me. I'd only been half-joking about being the last to know.

"And I know Dev's going to miss you, too."

"I sure am, Gabe. I'm glad you finally get to work on that book you've always talked about."

"Think of all the people I can libel." He laughed. "Especially the guy who wore a codpiece so he'd look bigger when he stood in front of female audiences."

Teresa grinned. "God, is that true?"

"It sure is."

"Who was it?"

"I don't know if I should tell you, Teresa. Might cut myself out of a book sale here. You have a credit card?"

She was delighted. "American Express Gold. Now tell me!"

"Okay." He nodded at me. "You know who it was, Dev?"

"Uh-uh. I'm as curious as she is."

"Downstate guy named Tim Aldrich. Real hot dog. I only worked for him because for some reason nobody could ever figure out he was against the war in Nam real early. Otherwise he was a reactionary bastard who thought half the population should be executed on general principle."

"And he really wore a codpiece?" Teresa said.

"He really did. But then so does Dev."

Teresa was in high spirits. "I doubt Dev needs one."

I made sure to give her a kiss on the cheek before I left.

CHAPTER | 18

"You sound tired, Dad."

"Down to the wire, sweetheart. I'm always like this about now in the campaign." I almost said, "You remember." But of course she wouldn't remember. She was the first among her friends to have parents who divorced. She'd been ten. Sometimes four, five drinks down I could still hear her weeping, begging us not to split up. I once broke three knuckles smashing my fist into a hotel wall when those images came back to me one lonely night on the road. "How's school going?"

"I'm taking theater as a minor, I've decided."

"Well, at least you don't want to be a rock star."

She giggled. "Why? Is that the thing now?"

"I was sitting around with some pols downtown the other night and four out of five of them said they had college-age kids who told them they planned to be rock stars. Theater sounds like a sensible decision compared to that. At least you could teach."

"You're getting carried away, Dad. My major is still poly sci."

"Maybe you should make your major theater and poly sci your minor."

"You're really down tonight. Are you all right?"

"Tired, I guess."

"You need a woman."

"Believe it or not, I'm getting ready, I think. Finally."

"I have a beautiful English professor here. She'd love to meet you. I even showed her your picture. She thinks you look sad and that intrigues her."

"Wait'll she sees me if we lose the election."

"Lake really caught up after that debate. Did anybody ever figure out what happened?"

"The official chemical report is that somebody slipped something called flunitrazepam in his Diet Pepsi. It's one of those date-rape drugs. And they figured out how to time it so it hit about fifteen minutes into the debate."

"I haven't seen that on the news."

"We just got word late today."

Cupping the phone: "Hi, Lauren. I'm just talking to my dad."

Her roommate. When she took her hand away I said, "Listen, honey, I'm beat. I just wanted to call and see how you were doing."

"I love you, Dad."

"I sure love you, hon." It was one of those moments when I wanted to just sit there and sob and I wasn't even sure why.

Ten minutes later I was in my boxers with a Robert Ryan picture on TBS. Of all the noir men, Ryan's my favorite. Melancholy and crazy at the same time. Feelings not unknown to me on my worst nights.

When the phone rang I almost decided not to answer it. But I had to answer it. Otherwise I'd lie there for hours wondering what the message had been. If it was important they'd make any words they left on the machine as cryptic as possible in case one or both of us had our phones tapped. I picked up.

"I know how late this is." Kate.

"This couldn't possibly be good news could it?"

"No, Bunny." She loved pet names. "But not bad news, either. I just found out that Gabe is leaving us and I wondered if you knew what it was all about."

"Who told you?"

"Gabe. On the phone. I called the office. He was still there. He was drunk but coherent. Some small press gave him a book deal?"

"Yeah, I know. Doesn't make sense to me, either."

Pause. "You know what I'm thinking . . ."

"Probably what I'm thinking."

"But I don't want to say it."

"Neither do I. But I may as well hang it out there. Maybe Gabe did the deed the other night."

"He had reason."

"He did indeed."

"And it wouldn't have been all that hard to do."

"No, it wouldn't."

"But it's not even good circumstantial evidence."

"I forgot you went to law school for a year."

"Two years."

"That's even worse."

She laughed. "You and lawyers."

"Can't live with 'em and can't live with 'em."

"Maybe we should just forget this call. I just can't believe Gabe'd do something like that."

"You ever hear anything about him confronting Warren?"

"Gabe? Confronting Warren? That's impossible. Gabe doesn't have it in him."

"Yeah," I said. "He sure doesn't." I let go a sigh. It sounded weary even to my own ears.

"Sounds like you need some sleep, Dev."

"I sure need something. I'll talk to you in the morning."

CHAPTER 19

I worked from my hotel room the next morning. I got Beth's phone number from Billy and called her at home. He said she was working the noon-to-eight shift at the beauty salon.

She didn't sound unduly happy to hear from me. But then she had no reason to. She was struggling with her feelings about her father—whom she probably loved about twenty percent less than she hated—and I was forcing her to walk into a past fraught with proof of his sins.

"You want something. I can tell."

"I need your help, yes. I'll pay you to help me."

"I don't want any money, Dev."

"Well, I appreciate that," I said. "Did you ever do any work on the computer for your father?"

"Sometimes. He couldn't keep secretaries. He always put the moves on them and they quit."

"I need to find his computer and his password."

"You want his computer?"

"I need to find out who he was working with the last couple of months. That may give us our killer."

"I guess I never thought of that."

"I know you have mixed feelings about him, but I'm sure you want to find his killer, don't you?"

"I guess I owe him that. He didn't deserve to die."

I was noble for once. I didn't tell her that there were a few hundred pols who might disagree with her on that. "No, he didn't. And that's why I need your help."

Long pause. "I have his laptop here in my apartment."

"Do you mind if I come over and get it?"

"I need to leave for work in an hour. Can you be here by then?"

I was there in forty-five minutes.

I went back to my hotel room and set off on a four-hour journey that took me through a list of Greaves's clients, which held several surprises. Some of the members of Congress who complained loudest about how corrupt and dirty politics had become had spent a lot of money, it seemed, with the wily Mr. Greaves. And from both parties. One page revealed a coding system that he used to hide various charges to his clients. They knew the code but were happy that nobody else did, the code hiding such items as escort services, gumshoes, even, in one case, a violent shakedown man well-known to the D.C. police. Greaves farmed out many of his smaller jobs. One of his principal tasks was collecting cash from firms that wanted favors from certain elected officials. This protected the client and the official alike. If a fall had to be taken, Greaves would take it.

Though no detail was given, there was an asterisked list of elected officials' names accompanied by specific dates and the names of cities. I was pretty sure that this was his private list of people he was blackmailing. He'd probably gotten to them the way he'd gotten to Warren. A man's opponent would hire him, in the course of his investigation Greaves would see an opportunity to do some blackmailing on his own, and he would keep everything from his client.

I was scouting names that recurred. Few did. You couldn't afford an association with Greaves. So you kept his employment brief. You wanted to put a nasty on your opponent's head. Once you got the nasty, it was bye-bye, Greaves. He hadn't been exaggerating when he said that he'd never been invited to a governor's ball or to a party on the Hill. If he looked like a pal of yours, the press would have you for breakfast, lunch, and dinner. You would be handing your opponent a formidable campaign issue—your association with Greaves.

In the last hour I found one name that appeared three times. I cross-checked the name with the dates of Warren's travels. I was able to match the name and date to the young woman who played the hotel maid with Warren.

The full name was listed only once. It was coded SC for secretarial services. From then on she went by the initials DF. Dani Fame. Though I knew that I was probably being my old judgmental self, I suspected that anybody with a name like Dani Fame was not (a) a police commissioner, (b) a NASA spokeswoman, or (c) a nun. She was more than likely a stripper who might be doing a bit of hooking on the side. This last suggested by the fact that she'd gone in and bopped Warren with no apparent qualms.

Thus began the last of my journey. Going online and scanning through all the entertainment ads and strip club listings in the city. At any other time the names would have been fun to just sit and ponder. Mona Mountains. Candy Crevice. Bambi Big. But this was work, and about halfway through the listings I considered the real possibility that one Dani Fame might well have moved on to other cities and other pols, possibly even at Greaves's suggestion. A million-dollar score, even for him, had to be a very stressful hit. If she was in the city, there was always the possibility that she'd somehow be identified as his associate. Even worse, he had to know that there was also the possibility that she might start blackmailing *him*. The name Dani Fame didn't inspire confidence where virtue was concerned. If you'll pardon me being judgmental.

Then I got lucky. I not only found where she was appearing; I found her website. Only one nudie shot, breasts only. But a good number of suggestive poses—anal, oral, doggy style, missionary position, and a couple that would require the skills of a gymnast and superhero to respond to effectively. The surprise was that she had, if you scrubbed away all the bad makeup, a very pretty down-home face. And the lively blue eyes reflected a real humor, as if she knew that this was pretty hokey. I suspected she was intelligent and maybe even fun to be with out of bed as well as in.

I took a break, did push-ups and sit-ups to clear my mind for another round at the computer. I ordered a burger and fries for lunch as my reward for being such a computer whiz and then went back to work.

Detective Sayers's idea that one of the staff had drugged Warren's drink was worth following up on. I'd had the same idea, of course, and so had Kate. But as I worked through page after page, I didn't see any name or code or symbols that resembled any staff member. I spent a lot of time matching names with codes. But it led nowhere.

And then it was there. On a page by itself. At first I didn't understand its significance. I hadn't known him. His name wasn't familiar to me. I'd probably heard it only two or three times in my life.

PHIL WYLIE

I was just about to try the next page when the name's importance became clear.

Of course. The man who'd worked all those years for Warren. The man who'd been truly beloved by what seemed to be the entire staff. The man who'd committed suicide a few days ago.

PHIL WYLIE

The rest of the page was absolutely blank. No code. No indication of what their business had been. No hint of any time frame.

PHIL WYLIE

From the little I knew about the man, he'd been something of a highbrow. Opera. Theater. Galleries. And a lover of beautiful, wealthy women, any number of whom had gotten quite silly about him. The "silly" thing being nothing but envy on my part. He'd probably been the guy I'd always *wanted* to be. I still thought the Three Stooges were funny, and the last beautiful wealthy woman I'd known had been the wife of a rich client of mine. She always said that I scared her.

PHIL WYLIE

Suddenly he wasn't just a name. He was a mystery. He'd killed himself. And now his name was appearing in R. D. Greaves's computer.

It was amusing to imagine these two doing business—the handsome, sleek Wylie and the coarse, shaggy Greaves.

I spent the next half hour reading all the local news stories about his suicide. Not a hint of foul play was suggested in any one of them. An unidentified woman, said to be "a good friend," told a reporter that she'd noted a certain despondency in him lately. "And he was almost never depressed. He was a pure pleasure to be with."

The stories confirmed my faded memories of his background. Moneyed family, Harvard Law, condo here, home in Aspen, political junkie who'd worked for Senator Nichols at one time. Twice married, twice divorced, a perennial on the local "Most Eligible Bachelors" list.

PHIL WYLIE

The Greaves connection just didn't make any sense. None at all.

And yet there his name was.

I poured myself a bourbon and drank it slowly, trying to think through all the angles the name presented. But by now I was too fatigued to puzzle them through. I even had to consider the possibility that the name meant nothing. That for some reason Greaves had decided to contact him but that the contact hadn't gotten him anything. The page was, after all, blank except for the name.

And then came the Edgar Allan Poe Hour and I nursed my familiar dusk depression for a time. Light a dirty city gray now in my windows. Roar of rush hour. Stream of limos disgorging people glittery or important enough to check into the hotel here. Voices of new guests in the hall. There would be fine food and finer sex for those lucky enough to indulge. Those insensitive swine. Did they think I *wanted* to be up here all alone? The only trouble with self-pity as a substitute for aerobics is that it doesn't do much for the waistline.

CHAPTER 20

Dani Fame's place of employment was the type of strip club where account executives took some of their best clients for a night out. Suits and ties everywhere, and the flashing of American Express Gold. Lap dances were discreetly limited to a large room off the main floor engulfing the runway. And even the strip music was reserved in its way, sexy but more artful in the way it enhanced the performances of the ladies.

And Dani Fame wasn't the only one of the ladies with a sweet face. In Leonard Cohen's *Beautiful Losers*, a character says that all he cares about is bodies: "I gave up fucking faces when I was fifteen." In college I thought that was a pretty nifty line. Maybe it's the glut of surgically altered features—whatever it is, I have a great appreciation for faces as well as for asses. Not great beauties necessarily. Just the nice, friendly girl-woman faces they were born with. And whoever chose these girls did, too. Their faces had youth, humor, intelligence. Like Dani Fame, they were in on the gag, too.

Purely as a matter of research, I sat slowly sipping a scotch and soda and watching the ladies for a half hour before I asked the waitress if Dani Fame would be performing tonight. "Gee, I'm not sure, I guess."

An obvious and awkward lie. I wondered what prompted it. This was between numbers. When the music hit she just shrugged her shoulders, tapped her ear as if she had been struck deaf by one of the dark gods, and walked away.

I finished my drink and walked back to the front door, where a Latin gentleman the size of a giant in a children's story was paid to decide who got in and who didn't—and who deserved punishment from his massive hands.

He didn't like me. Maybe he didn't like anybody. But for sure he didn't like me. I'd gotten no more than two words out when the bouncer said, "Not up for any bullshit tonight, man. You got a problem? Then that's *your* problem, not mine." He then pushed the door open for me, his expectation being that I would walk on out of there.

I decided to short-circuit the drama we were playing out, the drama that would likely end with him picking me up and hurling me out into the darkness.

"See this?"

"Yeah."

"One hundred dollars."

"I'm so stupid I don't know what I'm seeing?"

"I need to talk to Dani Fame."

"You and about a thousand other guys. She don't do lap dances and she don't go home with nobody afterwards."

"I just want to talk to her."

"And how would you do that, man?"

"That's where you and this hundred-dollar bill come in."

"Not enough, dude."

Oh, for those glorious days of film noir in the forties and fifties when a fiver would get you the secret to immortal life. Now a hundred dollars wouldn't buy you anything except the sneer of a bouncer.

"So what's the going rate?"

"Two hundred."

"And I get to talk to her?"

"And that's all you get to do. And you get ten minutes."

"I'd have to talk pretty fast."

"Make it three hundred and you get fifteen minutes."

He was running a business here.

"She happen to get any of this?"

"Half."

"She see a lot of men this way, does she?"

He shrugged. "Maybe."

If you were drunk enough and had cash enough in your wallet, this might be something to impress the client. Going backstage and talking to the stripper. Playing the man of the world. Oh, yeah, I know how to handle these situations. You'd likely have to keep the client on a short chain, otherwise he'd be trying to grope her. But after all the drinks and a lap dance or three, this would be an impressive evening capper for the right kind of client.

"You take the three hundred in pennies?"

"I don't know why you assholes think that's funny."

"You've heard it before?"

A sneering smile. "Ten times a month."

So much for my original and creative wit. I consulted my sacred wallet. I was down to four hundred-dollar bills. I pincered out two of them and lay them on the backside of the original hundred I'd shown him. "How's this?"

No magician ever made a stage prop disappear any faster. My three bills were long gone. He slipped his hand in the pocket of his extremely tight black jeans and dug out a cell phone. While he was punching in numbers, his biceps bulged in the narrow confines of his golden button-down shirt.

His near-twin appeared a few minutes later. They would have been twins except this guy was Caucasian. "Watch the door for me, Mickey. And make sure this dude don't wander back."

"Got ya. I owe ya anyway."

"I won't be long."

The bouncer and my three hundred dollars disappeared.

"He's a nice guy, ain't he?"

"Him? The bouncer?"

"Miguel is his name."

"You're talking about the bouncer?"

"Yeah. Miguel. What I just said, man. He's a nice guy. Why, you don't think so?"

"Well, I guess there are different ways of being nice." Maybe in Miguel's homeland, threats of violence are part of being nice. The same for shaking down rube customers when they ask to see one of the dancers. Nice.

Every once in a while, in the darkness redeemed only by the stage lights and the small bar on the far east wall, laughter would get so loud in the lap dance room it would drown out the music. Those had to be the right kind of lap dances.

Miguel came back. "Ten minutes."

"Hey, man, we agreed on three hundred for fifteen minutes."

"She's real busy tonight."

"I want a hundred back."

"You're gonna have to take it off me. And you try to put a hand on her, man, she calls me on my cell and I come back and break all your ribs."

"Your friend here was just telling me what a nice guy you are."

"He's young, man. He's never seen me in action. He won't be saying that after I get done with you, you step out of line tonight. And he can take you back there." He turned to the younger bouncer. "You take him back there, you hear?"

"Sure, Miguel."

"Get him out of my sight."

No doubt about it. There really are different kinds of nice. I just wasn't sensitive enough to pick up on Miguel's brand of it. There could be a whole new line of Valentine's Day cards. You bitch, you step out on me again I'll cut your fuckin' throat! Oh, yeah, and Happy Valentine's Day! (Be sure and make it a Miguel Masterpiece Greeting Card.)

The flashing runway lights. The conversations with the girls, the whistles and catcalls, all fell away after we closed the door behind us at the back of the place. Soundproofed. A long hallway with several doors on each side. Despite the claim that the girls weren't for sale, I wondered what was behind those doors. Could be a nice little hotel-style room. Not that I gave a damn. Or that I really gave a damn about most of the things that made me sanctimonious. I'd worn the label so long it was easiest to play to it.

Mickey knocked on a door at the far end of the hall. "Come in." Mickey pulled the door open for me then closed it after me.

I stood in a conventional dressing room. Three metal racks of various costumes, two plump overstuffed chairs, dozens of color photos on the walls of girls who'd appeared here. Some of them were likely dead now from drugs or beatings from boyfriends, husbands, or pimps. The dressing table was so long and wide you could play Ping-Pong on it. The folding chair, however, was slotted into a cut-out section close to the enormous round mirror where two spotlights from above gave the ladies maximum light. The rest of the table was cluttered with makeup bottles in dozens of sizes and colors.

Dani Fame wore a dark blue silk robe. She sat on the edge of one of the overstuffed chairs, a long white cigarette burning in the fingers of her right hand. She was innocent of makeup and looked as I had suspected she would, young and pretty in a simple but fetching way.

"Just so there's no misunderstanding, Mickey said you get ten minutes. I'm starting the clock right now."

"I saw a movie you made."

She knew what I was talking about. She didn't respond dramatically. But the mouth tightened with displeasure and the blue eyes showed unmistakable fear. "I've never made a movie."

"Oh, not the kind you see in a theater. Or even late at night on cable. But this was definitely a movie. Produced and directed by a Mr. R. D. Greaves."

She picked up an ashtray from the arm of her chair and obliterated her cigarette in it.

"You shouldn't smoke."

"I shouldn't do a lot of things."

"You shouldn't smoke and you shouldn't hang around R. D. Greaves."

"Maybe I should get Miguel back here. Tell him you grabbed me and tried to get me to do you."

"I'm carrying a Glock. If Miguel forced the issue, I'd shoot him and you'd be responsible because you told him a lie."

Now came the drama. She sprang up from the chair and clapped her hands together and said, "Fuck. He wanted me to do a bunch of them for him. With different men, you know. But that was the only one I did. And I felt real sleazy doing it. Prancing around here is different. When you come right down to it all it is is nudity. And there's nothing wrong with that. But ruining somebody's life . . ." She walked to the opposite chair. Sat on the arm. "How'd you find me?"

"Your name was in Greaves's computer."

Shaking her head. Looking up at me. "I suppose you're a cop."

"Uh-uh. I work for the man you were in bed with."

"The senator?"

"Yeah."

"As soon as it was over I started feeling sorry for him. I mean, he cheated on his wife with me, but a lot of men cheat. But they don't get blackmailed for doing it."

I sneezed. The powders, perfumes, and various kinds of makeup were shredding my sinuses. She got up and got me a few tissues from a box on the makeup table. When she turned around, her robe fell open. She was naked underneath. My kind of naked. Sweet little breasts and a modest crop of rust-colored pubic hair. "I guess it's working here. I'm not as modest as I should be."

"I appreciated the peek. I take it you don't have to have implants to work here."

"The two stars do. But the boss thinks it's a good gimmick to have the rest of us natural. I guess there're some guys who prefer us that way."

"Probably more than people realize."

But she was fully covered again as she sat down on the edge of the chair. "You ever really regret something you did?"

I smiled. "You mean when you're lying in bed at night alone and all the terrible things you did in your life come roaring back on you?"

She laughed. "Why don't we ever think of the good things in the middle of the night?"

"Maybe because we have consciences. A lot of people don't seem to these days." I hadn't been here five minutes and I'd just said something sanctimonious. "Of course I could be full of beans."

"You haven't asked me how I got hooked up with somebody like Greaves."

"You want me to?"

"Sure," she said. "I've got my excuse all ready."

"I'll bet I can guess. Money."

"I guess it wasn't that hard to figure out, huh? My husband. He's a junkie. There's a place in Canada that's supposed to be real good. But it's expensive."

"Sorry to hear that."

145

"My first husband was a drunk and this one's a junkie. The problem is when I fall in love I can't break away. As much as I love him, sometimes I wish I could."

The important question: "Did you have any idea who Greaves was working for?"

"You mean who was paying him?"

"Right."

"No. He got a call on his cell right before I went into the senator's hotel room. It seemed to irritate him, whoever it was. He said he didn't need any advice and that he'd been doing this for years and that the suggestion was stupid."

"But no name at all."

"No. I'm sorry."

Knuckled knock: "Couple minutes and you're up, Dani."

"Thank you." She said, "I need to put on my makeup. I hate makeup. But anyway you'll have to excuse me."

"Thanks for everything, Dani. Would you mind writing down your home phone in case I have any more questions?"

"You're not going to the cops?"

"Right now I don't see any reason to."

"Oh, thank you. And don't ask for Dani when you call. My real name's Sharon Bagley. How'd that look on a marquee?"

I f I ever write a book in my late years it'll naturally be about my time in politics. And the title will be *Always Bribe the Doorman*. I've never met one yet who wouldn't divulge the most dangerous of secrets if the money was up to his standards. Same with many cops, most corporate employees, at least half of all local pols, and— In other words, a good number of people will help you if the bribe is big enough. Shocking, isn't it?

The man with the red beard and the eye patch and the enormous nineteenth-century Austrian military coat that had spent at least one night in the shop of a Broadway costumer said, "That's very lower-class."

"A bribe is lower-class?"

"Do you have any idea who lives on these sixteen floors?"

"I know it isn't the pope. He's in the Vatican. And I know it isn't the president. They've got him in a psychiatric hospital now."

"Is your patter supposed to be funny?"

One of the clichés that's true is that the minions of the rich tend to be even snottier than the people who employ them. This six-six warrior was well spoken, his ruddy cheeks as frosty as his blue eyes, and his loftiness sort of humorous for a man who probably earned a nice, comfortable middle-class living, had a couple of kids and a pleasant but modest home, and yet saw himself as belonging to the elite.

"Well, I guess you're not interested in four hundred dollars." (For people who keep track of such things, when last seen my wallet was empty but for a hundred bucks. Thank God for ATMs is all I can tell you.)

We were inside the marble lobby of the building where Phil Wylie had once lived. About ten feet away, on the street, was where his body had hit. The street was busy now. He'd had his moment in the spotlight. I had a kind thought about him. Anybody who could win the affections of so many disparate staffers had to have been a pretty decent guy.

"But I'm curious."

I turned my attention back to him. "Yes?"

"Would breaking any laws be a part of this?"

"Marginally. But not likely."

"You'd have to do better than that." Irritated.

"I want to get into Mr. Wylie's condo for about fifteen minutes or so."

"Why?"

"I can't tell you why. I just need to check something."

"You're not going to damage anything?"

"No."

"Or steal anything?"

"Nope."

"How can I be sure of that?"

"Well, I guess you can't where the damage thing is concerned. But why would I want to damage anything? Do I look like a thug to you?"

"Yes, as a matter of fact, you do."

"Ah."

"Nothing personal."

"It never is. But as for stealing anything, you can shake me down when I come back down."

"That might work. But I'd need six hundred dollars."

"I have five hundred in my wallet. And unless you take credit cards, that's the best I can do."

"I suppose that might suffice. But I'd need to see the money before I made any judgment."

"Aren't you afraid one of your tenants might see me handing you the money?"

"Most of them are in bed by now or coming back here so drunk they wouldn't know what they were seeing."

"How low-rent."

"Yes," he said without humor, "isn't it, though?"

CHAPTER 21

The condo had the feeling of a museum. Artwork from half a dozen centuries lined the walls like a historical parade; the shiny hardwood floors were covered with Persian rugs and many derivations thereof; a grand piano sat next to a long vertical window through which came a mix of moonlight and streetlight. The silence was utter thanks to the construction of the building. The smells in the living room were those of the fireplace, wine, and marijuana; in the kitchen of good meals well prepared. Seven rooms cluttered with objets d'art of every kind— religious paintings, wallpaper, tapestries, glassware, ceramics, and many other things I was too ignorant to recognize for what they were.

Only when I walked near the doors leading to the balcony did I notice the evidence of the police investigation. The scuffs on the floor. The lingering scents of chemicals. Suicide investigations are also homicide investigations. Eliminate one and you have the other. The serology here is important. What were the contents of the victim's stomach, for one thing. Loaded up with drugs or alcohol may tell you something, for example. But there's always the possibility that the suicide was staged. A smart killer has been known to read a lot of material online looking for the best way to convince authorities that his man or woman did the deed themselves. I know of two cases where only after the medical examiner ruled suicide and the case closed was new evidence found that the person had actually been murdered. With as many friends and no doubt enemies as Wylie had had, the police would spend some time following up on any homicide leads no matter what the ME said.

I spent most of my time in the library because that was where his computer was. But that came to a quick dead end. The hard drive had been removed. I was assuming the police had taken it, but maybe not. The police or someone else had also emptied the desk drawers. I went to his videotape library, which didn't make sense. If he'd known anything about the blackmail tape, was he likely to leave it in full view on a shelf with his Fellini and David Lynch movies? I checked anyway.

I'd given the doorman my cell number. "It's been twenty-two minutes."

"I said 'or so.' "

"That's 'or so' to me."

"Five more."

"Two."

"Three."

"Two."

"All right. Two and a half."

"You've already used up the half."

I clicked off.

I know what you want here. The same thing I do. You want that last-second discovery where I shriek Zounds! And come bursting out of the condo like a madman, waving the blackmail tape and shouting the name of the person who'd not only hired Greaves but had also murdered him. And might have murdered Wylie in the process.

That happens in real life. Sometimes. This wasn't one of those times.

The final excitement for the long, long day and night awaited me back in my hotel room.

I'd been in just long enough to take off my coat when the phone rang. It was nearly eleven o'clock.

Billy said, half-hysterical, "Somebody broke into her place. It's a mess. Busted up all kinds of stuff."

He didn't have to say who he was talking about. Nor did he have to say why somebody had busted in. In fact he *couldn't* say why because, if he was telling the truth, he didn't know anything about the tape. Because presumably that's what the burglar had been after.

"Who the hell'd do something like this?"

"Nobody was hurt, Billy, right?"

"Well, no."

"It could've been a lot worse then."

"But what the hell would they expect to find here? In a neighborhood like this?"

"Junkies, Billy. They're desperate. They figure they can find a couple of things that'll help them make it through another day. Ask any cop."

"But then to go and trash the place on top of it. I just got here after work. They even left the door open."

"Maybe they heard somebody coming or something."

"Yeah, maybe. But you know this'll scare the hell out of Beth."

"It's up to you to convince her that she's safe there." And she would be. Tossing a place the way he or she had must have convinced them that no tape was to be found. Right now they'd be trying to figure where to put their skills to work next. They were working on a parallel course to mine. If Lake got it, the election was all over and Warren was finished forever. But there was the chance that it might come back to us via the blackmail route. Maybe they'd take Greaves's place in selling it to us.

I had all kinds of questions. Had they worked with Greaves? Were they freelancers who'd stumbled onto word of the tape? Or, the question I didn't want to ask myself, was one of our staffers involved?

"She said she grew up scared that somebody was going to kill her dad. And that they'd kill her, too. She said that when she was eight her dad and a guy opened fire on each other in their backyard. He got wounded pretty bad and the other guy got away. The weird thing is there's a part of her that still loves him even after all the crap he's done. I don't understand that, Dev. If my father was like him I'd never speak to him again. And even after her mother died, she stuck by him. But she was pretty pissed off at herself that she was at a movie when her mom passed away." He sighed. "I would've told R.D. to piss off a long time ago."

"Yeah," I said. "You'd think it'd work that way. But blood ties are hard to break sometimes. I always remember Jeffrey Dahmer's father showing up every day in court. Think of what he had to hear about his son. But he showed up anyway. I don't think I would've had that kind of nerve. Or love. Or whatever the hell it was. But he showed up anyway."

"I guess I'd never thought of it that way."

"I need some sleep, Billy. Just keep the doors locked."

"I bought a gun a couple weeks ago, Dev."

"Have you ever fired a gun, Billy?"

"I guess not."

"How about Beth?"

"I guess not, either."

"Then empty it out and put the bullets in one drawer and the gun in another."

"Maybe we'll need it."

"Trust me. In a panic you'll most likely shoot yourself or Beth."

"God, I was sort of looking forward to—"

"Bullets in one drawer. Gun in another. G'night, Billy."

CHAPTER 22

My mentor in the business was a former speechwriter for LBJ who quit over the Vietnam War early on and went into business looking for major pols who opposed the war as well. His name is Martin Steiner and he's still alive and well on his retirement farm on the coast of Maine.

As I sat in my office scanning the new internal polls, I thought of what Martin had told me about the situation I—and he, many, many times—was facing here.

Lake had the Big Mo right now. According to these internals he was two points behind. Which meant, all variables considered, that he was at least tied with us and maybe even ahead.

There are two kinds of TV spots you have to watch out for. One is when an issue breaks open suddenly. In Missouri a woman who'd been lagging opened fire in the last few weeks on her opponent's stand against stem cell research. The man had badly miscalculated the feelings of his state or he'd acted on principle. Whichever it was didn't matter. His stem cell stand cost him the election. Sometime issues work for you and sometimes they work against you.

The other is the attack ad leveled against your candidate. You have to determine quickly if the ads are hurting you. Some of the most virulent attack ads never gain much ground. If they're making a lot of noise but not doing much if any damage, you let it slide. But if they're damaging you, then you hit him five times harder than he's hitting you. Your oppo research people have a few juicy bits they've been pleading with you to use. You use them the last few weeks of the campaign—the Wild West of politics. There was a Midwest campaign in the forties in which one candidate (unfortunately on our side) continued to support his opponent by saying that he was sure the other man's campaign "was not being funded in part by the Greenleaf kidnapping case," a notorious recent abduction. That was the kind of support nobody wanted, especially since no reporter had ever suggested that kidnapping money was being used to support the opponent.

Lake's new hurried-up spot. (You can get them on the air in hours these days.) Medium close of Lake running around a track, good old all-American sweat streaming down his face, an American flag fluttering in the breeze behind him. Copy: "Sound of body." (And guess who wasn't sound of body?) "And sound of mind." (A magazine page that says: "Ever notice how many good-looking women work for congressmen? Suspicious?") Four quick stills of congressmen with true-blue babes who work for them. One of the stills was a pic of Warren at a bundle of microphones with Kate at his side. "And a man who honors his wedding vows." Medium close on Lake's kids and wife standing camera-frozen in front of an SUV with a dog hanging out the window that really looked like it needed to piss.

One way or the other they wanted to assault you with two facts. Maybe Warren was gravely ill and covering it up. And as for the good old family values—now that you mention it, Mr. TV commercial—maybe Warren, who'd been known to carouse in his early days, really hadn't *stopped* carousing. Look at some of his female staffers in Washington.

We'd have to decide fast how to respond to this commercial. I already had some thoughts. One of the oppo research guys had given me the thought two months ago. Then, I thought it had been out-of-bounds and might destroy us instead of Lake. Now I wondered. Now I had a notion of how we could use it without seeming to use it.

I called my secretary at the shop and asked her to get Warren's unabridged medical records and have them couriered to me right away. I didn't want them online. Docs knew better than to put anything menacing into a computer where important people were concerned.

Billy came in late. He had the haggard visage of a man who'd been worn out by alcohol, sex, or worry. We were alone in the office at the moment. "I couldn't sleep for shit."

"I kinda got that idea."

"Huh?"

"You look beat."

"Oh. Yeah. Beth's just as bad."

"Well, it's over."

"What if they come back?"

I had to play it confidently: "They won't."

"Easy for you to say, Dev."

"They know there's nothing there. Why would they come back? By the way, what did they take?"

"That's the funny thing. We went through everything carefully but nothing seemed to be gone. That's why we didn't call the cops. We figured we'd look ridiculous when they asked us what was stolen and we had to say, nothing."

"You're making my point for me, Billy. No offense, but you don't exactly live in luxury digs."

"Thanks."

"I didn't mean it that way and you know it. All I'm saying is that if they didn't turn up anything the first time, why would they go back for seconds?"

"God, I hope you're right." Then: "Man, did you hear the new Lake spot?"

"Got the copy on the TV spot. I'm sure they're just using the same track for radio. There's just one problem. They've got a family values radio spot implying that Warren's fly is still unzipped. If Warren's as bad off physically as they claim, how can he be schtupping all these women on the side? I mean, as much fun as sex is, it does require a little energy."

He had a nice rich laugh. "Thanks for trying to cheer me up. That's a good one."

"We've got a little ammo tucked away."

"The oppo people?"

"Yeah."

"What is it?"

I knew he'd take it personally. "I can't tell you right now."

"I guess I'm not important enough, right?"

"Shit, Billy, give me a fucking break, will you? Warren and I are the only two in the whole campaign who know what it is. If I'm snubbing you, then I'm also snubbing Kate and Laura and Gabe, too."

He shrugged. "Yeah. That's right. Sorry. I better get to work on his speech for tomorrow night."

No interruptions for the next half hour. I wondered if there'd been a nuclear attack that had knocked out phone lines. I wrote and three times revised the spot I had in mind for the big bomb. It was a risky idea. These kinds of spots are similar to the traps of declaring war. You never know where it will all end up. It could well do you in. Warren and I would both need some Xanax before the afternoon was over.

Laura came in late but appeared to be in control of whatever was troubling her so deeply. "Gym."

"It shows. You're more beautiful than ever."

"Sure."

"You're telling me you're not beautiful?"

"A bit above average is all."

But I could tell she was enjoying herself. It was nice to be with the real Laura again. The playful one. "Well, maybe a little better than above average."

"There we go, that old Laura arrogance I love."

"Not as beautiful as Kate."

"Matter of taste."

A giggle. "I can hear you saying the same thing to her only reversed."

"You think I'm insincere?"

"You're in politics aren't you?"

"Guess you've got a point there."

Then she, too, got down to work.

Last in was Gabe. In my idle times I thought about Gabe a lot. He still had the best reason that I knew of to do Warren in. Greaves had videotaped Warren only to get money. Gabe had a personal reason and personal reasons are usually the ones that burn hottest in the mind. Aging hippies don't like being in hock to peacock politicians.

"You hear that new Lake radio spot?"

"Yeah, Gabe, we talked about it a little earlier."

"To me he sounds like asshole number one."

"That's because he's on the other side. He's not saying anything that's not in the wind. Warren taking that tumble the other night left a lot of questions in people's minds."

If I wanted some kind of guilty expression, I didn't get it. He just said, "Maybe. But it still could come back to haunt him."

"It's got less than three weeks to do that."

He smiled. "You don't believe in happy endings?"

"There're a lot more happy beginnings than happy endings. The internals are in from yesterday and they ain't good."

"Lake picked up?"

"Picked up and at least tied us."

"Shit."

Then we were in the bunker. Phones, faxes, e-mails. And we all got them. Work became something you grabbed between responding to queries of all kinds from outlanders and barbarians who dared interrupt the holy process of getting our man elected. Insensitive bastards.

Somewhere during all this Kate came to the office. She'd spent the morning with Warren at a breakfast fund-raiser, then accompanied him on an inner-city school visit. Warren was very good with kids. And most of them took to him. If it were earlier in the election I'd have seen this visit as a photo op. But we were past that now. Now was the time when both sides took off the scabbards and went in heavy for disemboweling each other.

When it was just about time for a lunch break, Kate shared with us, as she did so often, new photos of her daughter, who, at three years of age, was a gleaming being of otherworldly splendor. Just like her mom. For all Kate's fashion and record of breaking hearts, only her daughter truly seemed to matter to her. But as wonderful as these moments were for Kate, they were miserable for me. I always thought of how much time I'd spent away from my own daughter and wife. The man who'd fathered Kate's child, whom she'd met on a fling in London, hadn't been the type she'd wanted as a husband or as a father. She had no resentment of him. She preferred being a single mother anyway.

After the photo display with all the oohs and ahhs, Kate came over to me at my desk. I'd turned back to work. She put her hand on my shoulder. "How're you doing?"

I put my hand over hers. "Better than I should be, given the internals."

She leaned down and kissed me on the cheek. "You're a good man, Dev. I wish you'd let yourself believe that once in a while. You judge a lot of people, but you judge yourself harshest of all." Then to cover that sticky compliment, she turned to the eavesdropping group and said, "Dev gave me one of his speeches yesterday about what a royal shit he is. But he's a good man, isn't he?"

Billy led the applause. My cheeks got warm. Laura knew how to whistle real loud and man she did so real loud right then.

"Thank you, everybody. And thank you especially to Kate, who bullied you into it."

Everybody laughed and then started hurrying out the door to lunch.

I called our oppo group and spoke with a man named Neal Walsh. He was the one who'd found our secret weapon. I'd asked him to get me printed evidence of what he was claiming.

"It wasn't easy, Dev. But I got the page we need."

"And there's no doubt about it."

"None. In fact I got two different pages. You'll see what they are. I'd rather not discuss them over the phone."

"Can you overnight them to me?"

"They're already on their way. You think you'll use them?"

"I'm drinking Maalox trying to decide."

"You run the idea past Nichols?"

"I'm meeting him for lunch in half an hour."

"It'd take some balls. But the beauty is, it's mixed in with so many other things, we can always claim that we didn't realize the significance of it. You know, we thought what was interesting was another bit of information on the page."

"Yeah. But my gut's still in knots."

"Well, you can always not use it. I mean, I know the risk here. Pols overshoot all the time and the public feels sorry for the other guy."

"Exactly. Anyway, Neal, thanks. Talk to you later."

I was getting ready to go when Teresa came in. She was wearing a brown suede coat, a white blouse, a rust-colored skirt, and brown leather boots that came to her knees. With her blond hair combed out, she resembled one of those older models who always attract me far more than the anorexic nineteen-year-olds.

"I stopped by for some flyers. I'm visiting hospitals this afternoon. There are voters there, too." She smiled. "I'll hit every floor except the morgue."

"Maybe a couple of them aren't really dead."

"I guess I don't have to ask about your taste in movies, Dev."

She walked around, touching desks and chairs as she did so. "God, Dev, how many campaigns have you and I been through? And you're not even forty-five yet. If you asked me for a count, I couldn't tell you. They all blur together."

"I'm starting to get that way myself. A blur. This is all I've done since I was in high school."

She smiled. "I remember you told me one night that you got into politics to get laid. Did that ever come true for you?"

"Only twice. And I had to use a gun and a bag of cash both times."

She smiled again. "That sounds like something Phil would have said. He knew how charming it was for a man of his looks and wealth to be self-effacing. When we first met him we both thought it was just an affectation. That he was really this arrogant rich guy who was sleeping his way through the Gold Coast. But when we got to know him, we knew he was being sincere." She tried to put a twinkle in her next words and she came close. But not close enough. "He was like you, Dev. He hated himself."

"I don't hate myself."

"Sure you do. You won't admit it to yourself, but you do. You think you're a very bad guy. And Phil was that way." She laughed. "My husband could use a little bit of that."

"And speaking of your husband, I need to go meet him for lunch." I got my coat. As I was shrugging into it I said, "You knew Wylie pretty well. Did he really have a reason to kill himself?"

"If he was drinking—which he did more and more I'm told, we'd lost touch with him after he left—he'd get despondent sometimes. Again it was mysterious to everybody around him. What could a man like him have to be despondent about? But it was always with him if you knew how to recognize it. People said he loved to laugh and he did, but when you watched his eyes they never seemed to be happy." She took a deep breath, exhaled. "That was a long answer and not helpful in any way. To answer your question, Dev, knowing what I know of him, he probably was suicidal deep down. But you make it sound as if it might not have been suicide. Or you're hinting at that, anyway."

"Not really. It's just that everything I've heard about him—all the glamour, I guess it just seems odd that he'd kill himself. That's all. If the police and the ME say suicide, so be it. What the hell do I know?"

She walked up to me and gave me my second kiss for the morning. Right about the same spot on the cheek Kate had planted hers.

I held the door for her and we walked out to our respective cars together.

Clean, soft breeze that touched the face lovingly, filled the nostrils with air that wouldn't dare be full of pollutants but likely was anyway.

"You have any idea who Wylie was seeing lately?"

She cast her eyes to the right of me, into the middle distance, as if balancing the effects of telling me or not telling me. "Maybe I'd better not say."

"Now there's an answer."

"What does it matter, Dev? He's dead. Why drag somebody else into it?"

"You're protecting somebody."

"Yes. Somebody I value very much." She moved toward her Volvo. "I need to go."

"Teresa, I'm not happy about this." Then I said, "Why did Phil and Warren have their falling-out?"

"To be honest, I'm not sure myself. All I know is that they went drinking one night and Warren came home with a bloody mouth. And the next time I saw Phil in the office he was packing up his things. And he had a black eye. I asked both of them what happened and they both said that they'd just had a disagreement over policy matters."

"And you believed them?"

"Of course I didn't believe them. But it didn't seem that important. People come and go all the time in political campaigns."

"But they were friends. Good friends, from what I hear. That's different than ending a business relationship."

She opened the door of her car. "Well, maybe you can get Warren to tell you the truth. I couldn't. And poor Phil's beyond helping anybody. He obviously couldn't even help himself. I'll talk to you later, Dev. I need to get going."

W hy did you and Phil Wylie part company?"

I thought he might gag on the Perrier he'd just started to swallow. He gulped it down and said, "We're falling behind in the election and you want to talk about Phil Wylie? What the hell's wrong with you?"

"Fair question, isn't it?"

"Sure it's fair. But since we met here at my club, I thought we were going to talk serious business. Not the past."

The club was one of those old-fashioned men's deals where all the leather chairs squeaked and the fireplaces blazed even in summer, the way Nixon's did in the White House of his years. Why Robert R. McCormick himself, old robber baron and longtime right-wing power behind the *Tribune*, had probably farted in the very chair I was sitting in now. I was having the salmon and Warren was having the chicken salad.

"So what happened?"

"What happened was very simple. We had a disagreement over policy."

"What policy was that?"

"What the hell is this, Dev?" A passing waiter gave us a look. Warren leaned forward, spoke in a lower voice. "It was over affirmative action. He thought I should push it harder, I didn't. It was a stupid argument, really. But it got heated and he said a lot of things he'd been wanting to say and then I said a lot of things I'd been wanting to say and all of a sudden it was all gone. Our friendship, our working relationship, and any trust we had in each other. It was painful as hell, believe me. I loved the guy and I think he loved me. He was my best friend. And it was over and it was irreparable and we both knew it. Now, is that good enough?" He sat back in his chair, angry. "It started out very much like this conversation, Dev. He pushed me too hard and I exploded and then I pushed him too hard and he exploded. Now, is that good enough for you?"

"Yes."

He laughed. "Good. Because I was about to put those vaunted boxing skills of yours to the test."

"Yeah, that's all we need this week, a candidate with a busted nose and bruises all over his face."

"You've got a lot of confidence for somebody approaching middle age."

"I still work out on the bag two or three times a week. I can handle myself. Nothing more. Now, let's get down to business."

The waiter came. We turned him down on dessert but both requested small glasses of wine. While we waited I reminded him of what Walsh had come up with a while back.

"I thought that was pretty much off the table. Too risky."

"All I'm saying is there's a way to bring it up."

"And how would that be?"

"His new commercial implies that you're not physically fit enough to stand for office. So we challenge him to release his total medical history. And we'll reveal yours."

He grinned. "That is some pretty devious shit."

I grinned back. "It sure is."

"You really think we should risk it?"

"If we make the challenge, then we have ourselves a new issue. We know he can't afford to release it because if he does, then his records will show that Mr. Family Values was treated for gonorrhea three years ago. So he can't release it, but we release yours and then start hammering on him twenty-four/seven to release his. And of course somehow somebody in our office will let it slip that Lake had a problem a few years back. And the press'll be all over him."

"I really appreciate how you fight for me."

I said it in such a way that he might finally understand it and quit flattering himself that I was his champion. "It's your voting record, Warren. Personally I think you're a piece of shit."

He gave a little start and said, "Well, fuck you."

"You lie to everybody around you. Nobody is ever sure what's going on with you. And I'm tired of it. Damned tired of it."

His face was flushed with real rage. "You think I have to sit here and listen to this shit?"

The passing waiter did a double take this time. So did the gentlemen sitting at the small tables in the center of the restaurant area.

Our voices dropped again.

"Yeah," I said, "I know you have to sit here and listen to this shit because I'm the only hope you have. And if you don't know that, you're dumber than I think you are. And that story you told me about Phil Wylie? No way, pal. I buy the fact that you had an argument that ended your relationship. But it sure as hell didn't start out over some small policy point. It was about something that meant something to both of you on a personal level. And I'm going to find out what it was."

"What if I insist that you stop wasting time on Phil?"

"Then fire me, Warren. I've already told you I'm quitting the day after the election. If you want to fire me now, fine."

"What the hell brought this on?"

"Are you crazy? What the hell do you think brought it on? I'm waiting for some piece of information you haven't given me to blow us out of the water. To hear it mentioned at a Jim Lake press conference. You just don't grasp the concept of trust, Warren. Not on a personal level or a professional one."

I stood up and threw my cloth napkin on the table.

"I've got things to do. I'll talk to you later. Right now I'm too sick of your face to sit here anymore."

CHAPTER 23

My cell bleated just as I swung into the headquarters' parking lot. Billy said: "Beth got sentimental this morning. Wanted to stop by her father's office. The woman down the hall, this exporter, said that she's been holding some of Greaves's mail. I put it on your desk."

"I appreciate that, Billy."

"I'm sorry I didn't tell you about Beth. It made me look bad when you just showed up at her apartment. I'm just glad I still have a job."

The mail turned out to be junk with one exception, a bill from something called Shadows, International, which was pretty damned melodramatic for a Chicago firm that had bought the cheapest envelopes and letterhead I'd ever seen. Not only was the paper already yellowed, it was also streaked down the center with a printing malfunction of some kind.

Shadows, International sent Greaves a bill for $425.17 for "client observation." That meant following somebody—hence, being someone's "shadow." Clever. The dates of this observation put the work done at two weeks previous. The "client" who was followed was not listed. The bill was signed in sprawling fashion by "Kenny Tully." I had no idea who he was, but now I had his address and phone number. The rest of Greaves's stuff I pitched in the wastebasket.

Gabe was first back from lunch. "Just caught the new Lake TV spot. You were right. Same audio track. Visually they're not that impressive."

"No, but they do the job."

"Lake's a scary guy."

This was something Gabe would say. But was he saying it now to cover the fact that he'd stiffed Warren's Diet Pepsi in order to stop Warren from winning?

He sat down at his computer.

I tried the number of Shadows, International. I got a scratchy answering machine. I didn't leave a name or number.

Laura came in wearing a new tailored gray coat. She even modeled it, giving us a twirl. "I decided to treat myself."

"You done good," Gabe said.

"You sure did."

"Thanks, guys. I appreciate being appreciated."

This should have been said happily. But the tone was somber. I remembered her tears of the other night. Her great grief. Because it had come so soon after Warren's performance at the debate, I wondered if she'd been part of it in some way. Stupid, yes, but I had to suspect everybody because only somebody close to Warren could have done it.

Midafternoon I got the call I'd been waiting for. Money was being sent from Washington to our campaign. We'd have what we would need for the final two weeks. I should have run down to the liquor store and come back with three bottles of champagne. But my lunchtime anger at Warren was still with me. I was sick of him. I just wanted the campaign to be over. I wanted him to win because people like Lake needed to be stopped.

By four o'clock I'd tried Shadows, International three times in all and got the answering machine each time. I was thinking of driving over there when our door opened up and Detective Sayers, the dapper black gentleman, walked in. He didn't need to say anything. He just nodded at me. I got up and walked over to the coat tree. "I'm finishing up for the day," I told everybody.

They were all watching Detective Sayers. They didn't know his name, but they certainly knew his profession. He had that unmistakable cop air of superiority and impatience. I followed him out the door. "Anyplace we can sit down and have some coffee?"

"Right down the street."

The coffee shop closed at six. They didn't get a rush-hour business. The counter man was already cleaning the grill. The place had that lonely closing-up feeling.

Sayers had coffee and a bagel. "This'll be dinner until about nine o'clock. You having anything?"

"Just the coffee. I'll be having a five-star meal in about forty-five minutes or so. Unless you're planning to put me in jail."

I assumed that would draw some kind of humorous response from him. It didn't. And that bothered me.

We started in on our respective coffees and he said, "How long have you known Nichols?"

"Any particular reason you're asking?"

"You know how uniformed people have ticket quotas? They have to hand out so many for a time period?"

"Uh-huh."

"Well, detectives have question quotas. We have to ask so many a day or we get our asses kicked when we get back to the cop shop."

"Makes sense to me. And you guys should get your asses kicked a lot more than once a day."

"So how long have you known him?"

"He's been a client of the place where I work for a long time. Ten years at least. I've worked with him off and on for five, six years. Why?"

"You trust him?"

"He's a politician."

"That's cute but it's not an answer."

"I trust him, yes. I wish I knew why you were asking me these questions."

"You were with him in the dressing room when his drink was queered, right?"

"I was with him in the dressing room. We're assuming that that was when the stuff was put in his drink. Around that time. Maybe a little bit before."

"You got any idea who might have put the stuff in there?"

"Afraid not."

"You could've put the sedative in his glass."

"Yes, I could've."

"But you didn't, right?"

"Right."

He finished his coffee. He was a bit loud about it. He went "Ah!" and smiled. "This is some of the worst coffee I've ever had."

"We don't come here for the coffee."

"Oh? Why do you come here then?"

"The atmosphere. Don't let all the wobbly furniture and the greasy walls fool you. This is a high-class joint."

"It is, huh?"

"Just don't use the toilet."

"Bad?"

"So bad that people go in there and are never heard from again."

"I'll remember that."

He spoke without taking his eyes off me. "Way I've got it figured, it was somebody on the staff put that sedative in his glass. You considered his staff?"

"Of course."

"You got any leads?"

"Not so far."

"Who looks good for it?"

"Nobody."

"Maybe you don't know the staffers well enough."

"Pretty well."

"Background checks?"

"Yep. Or they wouldn't have been hired."

"Grudges against Nichols?"

"Distinct possibility. Lots of hurt feelings in campaigns. But nothing stands out at the moment."

"You ever consider the possibility that Nichols himself put the stuff in his Diet Pepsi?"

Fastball right across the plate. Breathtaking in its simplicity and fury. It stopped me clean and cold. I'd never even considered that possibility. "I don't believe that for a second."

"We got a tip."

"My advice is burn it. It's bullshit. Why the hell would he do it?"

"The race was tightening."

"Not that much."

"The race was tightening and he figures he can nail Lake with queering his drink. But it doesn't work out that way. Lake becomes the hero. But now there's not jack Nichols can do about it."

"Agatha Christie."

"What?"

"That's an Agatha Christie plot. I don't remember which one. But I've read all of her books and I'm sure she used that same trick in one of them."

"Maybe I should read her."

"Mostly I read noir. But Agatha's fun every once in a while."

"This sounds like the literary society. How about you tell me what you think about my idea. And don't just say it's bullshit."

I finished my own coffee, carefully setting the cup down. I cleared my throat. I stared across the table at him. "He didn't do it. Too risky and he's very conservative when it comes to risk. And he'd screw it up."

"What's that mean?"

"He's not a competent man. He was raised with money. He never had to learn how to survive on his own skills. If he was to do something like this, he'd have to have somebody help him with it. He's not stupid but he is lazy. He'd have to have somebody figure out which kind of drug to use. Then he'd have to have somebody figure out what the best way was to make everybody else think somebody had put it in his drink."

"Maybe he had help."

"If you mean me, I like my job too much. Too many things wrong with a plan like that. Bound to come undone somewhere along the line."

"There are plenty of dudes floating around who'd help him for some serious money."

"Right. But we're back to risk. He gets help like that, he instantly sets himself up for blackmail. You don't meet a high class of people in that particular trade. I don't suppose you'd tell me where you got this tip?"

"As a matter of fact, I will. Came to me in a letter. Unsigned, of course. It was just off-the-wall enough that I thought I should look into it."

"And now you have."

"And now I have."

"So you're not going to worry about it anymore?"

He smiled with those big white teeth of his. "Of course I am. I think it's a very interesting idea."

CHAPTER 24

I drove from there to the co-op building where Phil Wylie had lived. A black doorman was on duty tonight. He was middle-aged, but from the appearance of his graying hair and the broken ridge of bone above his eyes and the condition of his nose, his boxing days had likely left him capable of taking care of himself even today. He wore dark blue woolen gloves that matched his uniform coat. I couldn't get a glimpse of his knuckles. I asked him where the other man was.

"Night off."

"Be back tomorrow?"

He nodded. He watched me carefully. "Cop?"

"Pardon?"

"You a cop?"

"Long time ago. Military intelligence."

"Thought so."

"Don't hold it against me."

He had a chesty, full laugh. "I'll try not to."

"You interested in a little money on the side?"

"I don't have a police record if that's what you're asking. And I plan to keep it that way."

"Did you know Phil Wylie?"

"Mr. Wylie? Sure. He was a very nice man. He gave a damn about people. My little granddaughter, she got sick and her mama didn't have no insurance, he picked up the hospital bill. About four thousand dollars. Not many folks'd do something like that."

Wylie's death was beginning to have its effects on me. I was getting to know him through the people who'd loved him. "He must've been a damned good man."

"He was. Half the people who work here went to his funeral." He allowed himself a quick smile. "Some of the people in this building, they die and we want to celebrate instead."

I realized that I should start carrying my wallet in a holster. Easier to get to. I slipped a hundred-dollar bill from it and offered it to the man.

"What's this for?"

"I want to know about his visitors."

"What visitors?"

"Anybody you saw come here more than two or three times."

"I only work here two nights a week. Rest is days."

"Then tell me about the two nights."

"This what you gave Ralph?"

"Ralph?"

"The other doorman."

"I gave him a little more."

"How much is 'a little'?"

I took out another hundred. "How's that?"

"Passable."

"Tell me about his guests."

Before he could respond, a limo pulled up out front and dispatched a young couple who were trying awfully hard to be Scott and Zelda. They were both drunk and giggling and each waved a bottle of champagne. They stumbled and staggered through the front doors. By this point the young man, who had his hair greased back and his white tuxedo shirt covered with red lipstick wounds, kept trying to kiss her exquisite neck, but her fur wrap kept getting in the way. I wanted to call PETA and have them beat the shit out of these two on general principle. They stumbled on across the echoing marble floor to the elevators. If they'd seen us they'd decided we weren't worth acknowledging. More likely they were too drunk to see anybody who didn't appear regularly in their mirrors.

"I'll bet they're your favorites."

"Believe it or not, they're pretty decent compared to some of them."

"There're worse?"

"You kidding? Wait till you meet the Sullivans."

"Bad?"

"She always tells me it's nice to meet 'a colored man who knows how lucky he is' to have a job."

"I see what you mean."

Now he gave the subject of Wylie and his visitors some thought. "Last month or so, this one guy kept showing up a lot. He didn't belong here."

"What'd he look like?"

He gave me two sentences. He gave me R. D. Greaves.

"He stay long when he came here?"

"Once he stayed over an hour. Most of the time it wasn't that long."

"Anybody else?"

And then he said it. I knew right away the who of it. What I didn't know was the why. And then I remembered the night in the office when she'd been sobbing but wouldn't tell me what was troubling her.

"She was a real babe. Real North Shore. A very classy number."

"She here a lot?"

"Just about every night I was."

"She stay long?"

"Most of the time overnight. I'd leave at six when the day man came on and she'd be coming down in the elevator about then."

Laura and Phil; Phil and Laura. Nothing wrong with that. Perfectly fine. Office romances happen all the time. And nothing sinister about it, either.

Then why did it seem sinister to me?

As soon as I got back to my car, I called her on my cell. I got her voice mail.

K ate was on the phone when I got back to the office. I'd just sat down when she said good-bye and hung up. "I hear we got the money."

"Yeah. I don't know what moved them all of a sudden."

"Would you like to see Jim Lake in office?"

"You've got a point there."

She went over and got her coat. "I left a number there. A man called twice for you. He sounded sort of—agitated."

"He leave a name?"

"You won't believe it. Shadows, International. He sounds short."

" 'Sounds short.' "

"Yes. It's this ability I have. Even over the phone I can tell if a man is short. There's just this aggression in their voices. Sometimes it's very subtle and almost nobody else can hear it."

"Like a dog whistle."

"If you insist," she laughed. "It's just like a dog whistle."

I dialed the number as soon as she was gone.

"Shadows, International. Tully speaking."

And damned if he didn't sound short.

"Mr. Tully, my name—"

"I know who you are. I've got caller ID."

"Good for you."

"Kind of a wise one, are you?"

"That's what they tell me."

"You called three times. I wondered why."

"You sent R. D. Greaves a bill for services rendered. I wondered if you'd tell me why."

"Hell, no, I wouldn't tell you why."

"That's what I figured. Is there a bar near where you are?"

"Lots of them. Why?"

"I've got three hundred and fifty dollars in my wallet that I've really got to get rid of because it's too heavy to carry around. I've also got a Glock nine-millimeter in case anybody might get the idea of taking the money from me before I'm willing to give it. But you sound like a deserving type of guy. So why don't we have a couple of shooters and see if we can do a little business."

"Five hundred would interest me a lot more."

"For five hundred I'd want a pretty full story. Not just a brief explanation. I'd want to know who you were following for him and why."

"What if the person I was following doesn't have anything to do with what you're looking for?"

"Then I'm out the three hundred and fifty dollars I'm going to give you."

"Five."

"Four."

"Four fifty."

"Four ten and fifty cents."

"What are you, some kind of asshole?"

"Yeah, but I've never figured out exactly what kind."

He named a bar. Forty minutes later I pulled into the parking lot.

Middle-management white-collar employees. More upscale than I would have figured for Mr. Tully. He wasn't hard to find. The shortest man in the place. Plus an idiotic trench coat with enough epaulets, flaps, and buttons on it to embarrass even real secret agents.

He was chatting up a very nice-looking blond woman who towered over him at five-eight or so. A real Amazon compared to his five-five. Her dark eyes kept furtively searching the long, narrow room. She wanted to be rescued.

"Excuse me, ma'am," I said, stepping up to them. "This man recently escaped from our psychiatric hospital and, as charming as he is, I'm afraid we'll have to take him back there for another round of two hundred electroshock treatments."

"My faith in God has been restored." She smiled. And fled.

"You've got a way with the women, I see."

"You prick."

He was a munchkin. The real kind. Sort of a Kewpie doll–face male version and short arms that made long-sleeved shirts and jackets hard to buy. "She was going home with me."

"Yeah, I noticed that."

"What? You think I don't get my fair share of pussy?"

"Why're we having this conversation?"

"Because you chased off my babe."

"Tell you what. Let's find a booth and I'll buy you a couple of drinks."

"Oh, no, man. You chased off my woman for tonight. But you're not gonna chase off my regular fee."

"Your fee? For what?"

"For talking to me. That comes extra."

Anita Baker came on the sound system. I'd had a music crush on her back in the eighties and early nineties. I wanted to sit in a booth by myself and think about the impossible woman I was going to meet real soon now. Instead I had to deal with this sharpie. "So I pay you a fee up front even though I'm not sure you have any information that would be of any interest to me."

"Hey, you called me. So if you want a sit-down here it's the same as a sit-down in my office. Seventy-five an hour. And that's seventy-five even if you get up and leave in five minutes."

"You're sort of like a shrink."

Somebody was having a birthday. A group of drunk men and women laughed their way through "Happy Birthday," drowning out Anita Baker. Nothing good lasts very long.

"You mean I don't even get one freebie?"

"Man, this is what I do for a living. No freebies."

We took a booth. A good-looking middle-aged waitress came over and took our orders. Tully said, "I don't see no ring on your lovely hand."

"My wedding ring's so big, it's hard to carry around."

"You're kidding. You're not married."

"You a psychic?"

"I just have married radar. You know, like gaydar. Only it's about which babe is married and which isn't."

"You should be more like your friend there."

"Yeah?"

"Yeah. And not pester the waitresses."

As soon as she left, I said, "Another triumph."

"Some of 'em you have to work awhile. But eventually most of them come around."

"Yeah, hit 'em with a crowbar, they'll give in every time."

"You're so smart, let's see your money."

I hadn't kept track of all the bribes I'd delivered in the past few days. The amount had to be twelve hundred or around there. Our accountant would frown and sigh. She was not only very good at accounting, she was even better at frowning and sighing, especially when it came to the sloppy way I kept track of things.

I laid out a one-hundred-dollar bill. I didn't have anything smaller. "Bonus."

He shrugged. "I'll call the networks and let them know what a high roller you are."

"Did Phil Wylie hire you?"

"You're with Nichols, right?"

"Right."

"I Googled you."

"Good for you. Now answer my question."

"Greaves hired me to help him with the Wylie case."

"To do what?"

"To shadow a couple of people."

"A couple meaning two?"

"A couple meaning two."

"Do I get the names?"

"That's where the negotiations start."

"I could always come across this table and pound your face in. Would that start the negotiations?"

"I pack heat."

"Mickey Spillane, 1948. That's an old song, pal. I pack heat, too. But I'd hate to mess up this pretty booth with your blood."

"Two thousand dollars for the reports I gave to Wylie."

"Believe it or not, I don't have two grand on me."

"I want it in cash so there's no way to trace it to me."

"You don't like to pay income tax."

"Not only that, but selling this kind of thing, this gets around I have to think of my reputation. People might get the idea that I'm double-dealing them. You know, I get information on one guy and he pays me. And then I turn around and sell the same information to his enemy. That could put the hurt on my business."

"And trench coats don't come cheap."

"You don't like my trench coat?"

The waitress came with our drinks. "I told my friend here that if I worked on you long enough you'd go home with me."

She smiled at me. "He really say that?"

"Well, he didn't say it specifically about you. He said it in a more general way. But you were included."

"He couldn't get me to go home with him if he had an Uzi and a bag of gold coins."

Shadows, International smiled. "You'd be a challenge but I think I could swing it."

She shook her lovely head in disbelief and walked away.

He said, "Bitch. She just wanted to embarrass me in front of you. Wanted to make my work harder for me. Wants me to work real hard for my nookie tonight."

Say what you want about delusional people, they're an awful lot of fun to listen to sometimes.

"Okay, rock star, let's get serious here. I can have the money for you tomorrow morning. How do I get it to you?"

"You leave it at the front desk of your hotel?"

"That sounds easy enough. And you leave the reports for me when you pick up the money. And you'll be damned sorry if the reports aren't there."

"Man, you think I'd try and screw you or something?"

"Gosh, no. A man of your integrity?"

"So get outta here and let me work. That waitress don't want to go home with me, I'm sure I'll find some broad who will."

"Probably a line around the block there'll be so many."

He didn't like me much, but then the feeling was completely mutual. He worked both sides of the street and didn't make any secret about it. There are some things you just don't want to know.

I bought a Repairman Jack paperback in the hotel lobby. I'd been reading F. Paul Wilson since I was in college. The Jackster was his greatest creation. I liked the idea of somebody who helped people just for the sake of helping rather than somebody who did good for self-aggrandizement. Superman kind of digs his power a little bit too much, don't you think?

I read fifty good pages. I turned out the light, expecting to get to sleep. But that didn't happen until I spent a useless half hour on a lot of what-ifs, a lot of dead ends, a lot of pointless speculation. Who'd killed Greaves? And where was the tape?

I finally got to sleep a little before midnight, but it didn't last long. The phone woke me at 12:49, according to the nightstand digital clock. My first thought was, as always, about my daughter. The parental terror that something had happened to the most precious person in your life. I rolled over, reached long, and grabbed the receiver.

"Hello."

The voice was being filtered through some kind of electronic device. No gender. The words so muffled a few of them were lost to me. Like a bad recorded message.

"I'm picking up where Greaves left off. I have your tape and I want what Greaves wanted for it. One million dollars. I want it at nine P.M. the day after tomorrow. You'll leave it in your car in your hotel parking lot. I'll"—muffled—"in the front seat." Muffled. "There will be no other contact. If you cheat in any way the tape will go to a TV station immediately."

I hadn't even had time to wake up properly. I was in a dream state for a few minutes after the call. I knew the call was real, but it remained unreal somehow. I went to the john and took care of myself and then washed my face in icy water.

My guess was that I'd just been contacted by the person who'd hired Greaves. Maybe Greaves had passed the tape off before he'd been killed, making the search by at least two parties useless. Or maybe the person who'd just called, Greaves's boss as it were, had been unhappy with Greaves and had killed him and taken the tape.

Whatever the case, we were back where we started. The tape in exchange for one million dollars. The way it was set up, they saw the money before I saw the tape. If the money wasn't there, the tape wouldn't be there. That simple.

I slept. Maybe it was pure escape. A retreat from reality. But I slept straight through until eight-thirty and even then I didn't want to get up, could have slept a few hours longer.

B y the time I got to headquarters, the staff had been at it almost two hours. I slipped into desk position and went to work immediately. The third new e-mail I opened was from a friend of mine at a large TV station. He said that there would be a new Lake spot premiering at eleven A.M. our time, that the substitution was made early this morning. Which had an ominous sound to me.

The spot would air half an hour from now. Gabe and Kate were the only two people in the office at the moment. I told them what was coming up.

"Maybe their oppo research people found something," Gabe said. He sounded properly nervous. But there was amusement in his eyes. Though he might pretend otherwise, he'd be happy to see Warren brought down, even if it meant that Lake would win.

Kate said, "Don't we have anything, Dev? We really need to fight back with something powerful. Everybody knows that Lake gets a lot of money under the table from lobbyists."

"If that was a crime," I said, "you couldn't get a quorum for a vote in Washington. We need something a lot stronger, something that's unique to Lake."

"Any idea what he came up with?" she asked.

"Wish I did."

"This could blow us right out of the water." The glee in Gabe's voice was unmistakable.

"I know, Gabe. You're going to start crying any minute now."

"Hey, what's that supposed to mean?"

"Forget it."

I turned around in my chair, faced my screen, and went back to work. Difficult to concentrate. Most politicians come to think they're irreplaceable. That's why term limits have never gone anywhere. The divine right of kings has nothing on most pols in our country. They have manipulated the laws so that getting rid of them is virtually impossible. It can be done, but it usually takes a major seismic shift in public attitude to do it. And it usually comes as a surprise late in an election cycle. The last debate started us on our downward slide. And we hadn't recovered yet. Maybe this new commercial would contain a charge that would knock us even lower.

"It's almost eleven," Kate said. "I'll turn on the TV."

The three of us grabbed quick coffees and stood in front of the TV, pagans before a false god.

The spot was scheduled for 11:08, premiering on a statewide talk show that had a large audience.

The first seven minutes were spent with the host asking two female reporters which candidate—Nichols or Lake—held the most appeal for women. One of them laughed and said, "Neither." Then they got down to some serious assessing of the implications in the question. Both were manly men, though Lake was the manliest. Both were intelligent men, though Nichols was the most intelligent. And then came the health question. One of the reporters said that that was "the wild card." And the other agreed. "I really felt sorry for Senator Nichols and what happened to him at the debate. But it made me wonder about his fitness to serve." That was reporter one. Reporter two said: "He just looked so old and frail suddenly. That's probably being unfair. You can look old and frail when you're eighteen—if you're sick enough. But this was the image that a lot of people took away from that debate. That here was this old man being helped by this younger, more vital man. This is one of those times when health really becomes an issue."

The spot opened on a long shot of a man swimming laps in an Olympic-size indoor pool. We go into a medium close shot of the man swimming toward us now. The man is Jim Lake. We cut to Lake rising out of the water like a sea creature, water pouring off his tight, muscled body. And the voice-over accompanying all this: "A swimmer in college. A winner in Congress." And then suddenly a long shot of Lake, surrounded by a six- and seven-year-old mixed-race group in swim trunks on the edge of the same pool, Lake demonstrating swimming strokes. Now they are all in the pool, Lake swimming slightly ahead of the pack, still showing them how to swim. "A family man, a fit man, a man who never tires of fighting for the right things, the good things in American life." And we end on a freeze-frame of sea creature Lake in all his trim, muscled glory coming up out of the pool again.

"Motherfucker," said Laura, who'd come in just as the spot had started to play.

For half a minute or so, hers was the only comment.

Gabe said, "I thought he played football in college."

"He was out one year because of an injury, so he swam," Kate said. "What'd you think, Dev?"

"Corny and obvious, but it keeps on message that Warren is a broken-down old man too tired to do anybody much good."

"That's such bullshit," Teresa said, coming through the door. "I watched it out front with the volunteers. I should do a spot about how virile he is."

"Yeah," I said. "If you could work the phrase 'sex machine' in there a couple of times, that'd be helpful."

Teresa blushed, as if just now realizing what she'd said. "Well, you know what I mean. This is ridiculous. Somebody put something in his drink. He's fine now."

"Do you think they'll stay with this health thing for the rest of the campaign?" Laura asked me.

"Unless we can force them off it. Put them on the defensive."

"Is that possible?" Kate said. "Do we have anything that could do that?"

"Maybe," I said. "I need to talk to Warren. Anybody happen to know where he is?"

Teresa said, "He's between TV interviews. He should be back here in another half hour or so."

"Great. Thanks. Guess I'll get back to work."

Teresa came over and said, quietly, "We could lose this, couldn't we, Dev?"

No point lying. I nodded.

"They blame him for that stupid drug he took. It's not fair."

"No, it isn't. But it's politics."

Then she said what was *really* on her mind. "Maybe we should've accused Lake right away. You know, of hiring somebody to put the drug in the drink."

Her voice still wasn't loud, but it was enough that everybody heard her. Everybody started paying attention to the conversation now. Everybody knew what she was saying. That this was my fault because I'd told Warren we shouldn't make any kind of accusation until we could prove it absolutely.

"If you're asking me if I handled it correctly, Teresa, maybe I didn't. Maybe I should've suggested that we go on the attack. Make Lake the bad guy right away. But we had no evidence—and we still don't."

"People make unsubstantiated claims all the time, Dev."

"Al Sharpton comes to mind. I don't think I want to throw in with him, do you? Bush, Cheney, people like that? They made a lot of unsubstantiated claims, too."

"You're being silly. If you think you made a mistake, you could at least admit it."

Now she was the typical political spouse. Protecting her husband from the stupid consultant whose stupid mistakes were about to deprive the nation of one of its finest leaders. I'd made mistakes in my time and had apologized for all of them. But I didn't see this as a mistake. Lake had cleverly shifted the subject from the drink Warren had taken to the general subject of Warren's health. The only tactic we could have used was a dubious accusation.

"Well, I'm not happy about this, Dev. I want you to know that."

"I'm not happy about it either, Teresa. And believe it or not, I think there's a way to respond to it. All I need is Warren's approval."

Tears now. "I just hope you know what you're doing. We're a part of Washington now. We have a beautiful home and a lot of important friends."

And a lot of important friends. When senators are forced from office, many of them stay in D.C. and make enormous amounts of money as lobbyists. But there is no amount of money that can compensate them for the power and prestige they've lost. There are only a handful of United States senators. Except for the president and the vice president, there is no more significant role you can play in our government. Each man or woman is sought out by powerful people from around the world. People who want favors. People who give favors. No lobbyist ever gets that kind of treatment.

"I guess I'd better go," Teresa said. The tears were flowing openly now. I wasn't angry, I was just disappointed. I'd always felt that she hadn't been seduced by all those dos in Georgetown. All those dinners for visiting potentates. All those evenings at the White House. But I'd been wrong.

"Sorry you had to go through that, Dev," Laura said.

"Wasn't so bad."

"That's a side of Teresa I've never seen before," Kate said.

"She's a limo junkie. She digs the red carpet," Gabe said.

"She wants her husband to win, Gabe. Nothing wrong with that."

"C'mon, Dev, they're both addicts and you know it. They dig the red carpet and all that shit."

"You think Lake would be any different?"

"We're talking about Nichols. Not Lake."

Nichols, I thought. The guy who kept loaning you money when you needed it for your stupid gambling problem. The guy who could've ended your political career with one phone call. The guy who at least votes the right way ninety percent of the time. I was sick of Warren, but Gabe's attack was hypocritical and annoying.

"You ever think there'll be a day when you help put somebody in office you actually have respect for, Dev?"

"I guess you don't want to let this go, do you, Gabe?"

"It's a fair question."

"Give it a rest, Gabe," Laura said.

"It's a stupid question anyway," Kate said.

"What's so stupid about it? Just because you people don't mind working for whores—"

I forced a smile. "And here I thought that *I* was the sanctimonious one, Gabe. We're human. That's what you're not factoring in here. If I ever got to be a senator, I might be the biggest whore who ever hit Washington."

"That's not true, Dev," Kate said, "and you know it."

"No, I don't. We've all seen it happen to people we thought we respected. They start living with all those privileges and perks and having their staffs do everything for them—I don't think you can predict how most people would react."

"There're a few you can predict," Laura said.

"Yeah, a few. Just a few. Men and women who don't get their heads turned by all the fuss made over them. But everybody else—" I shrugged. "I need to get back to work."

Over the next half hour I wrote copy for the spot that would respond to the health issue. Then I wrote a statement that Warren would give at his appearance at a luncheon for retired party officials. The press would be expecting a droner. Few pols used an appearance like this to make news. We didn't have much choice. I did all this presuming that Warren would agree with it. One look at Lake's new commercial would convince him that we needed to move quickly. Especially given what oppo research had been able to find out about Lake. All this was predicated on the hope that they weren't holding back any oppo material of their own. The conventional belief being that any major attack coming in the last two weeks of the campaign was virtually impossible to counter. You just didn't have the time to make your case effectively.

Warren came in just after noon. He said, in a tone as harsh as I'd ever heard him use, "Everybody out except Dev. And I mean now."

When we were alone, Warren said, "Let's nail his balls to the wall."

"Great," I said. "But now we have another problem."

"The bearer of good tidings, eh?" He was ready to be angry.

"We've got another blackmailer in the picture."

CHAPTER 25

☆ ☆ ☆ ☆ By midafternoon every news source available to us, in-
☆ ☆ ☆ cluding all the cable news outlets, was carrying the
☆ ☆ ☆ ☆ story of how Senator Warren Nichols, slipping in the
☆ ☆ ☆ polls, had made available online his complete medical
☆ ☆ ☆ ☆ records dating back to age sixteen. We'd stored them this way in case
we ever needed them. And now we needed them.

That was point one of his attack. Point two was that he was challenging Congressman Jim Lake to do the same in the next twenty-four
hours. Everything in his medical history.

Point three was an ominous but vague suggestion that Nichols's
drink had been tainted by "forces against my voting record," which he
then listed highlights of. He emphasized how hard he'd fought for
both the middle class and the working class. And how he'd managed
to improve the lot of the working poor, "folks who Jim Lake once
called in one of his more reckless and inhumane moments 'dispos-
able.'"

He concluded with, "I get a physical twice a year at Walter Reed.

I'm healthy in every respect. And I've never suffered from any disease that would embarrass me."

I'd rewritten that last line five or six times. I'd wanted to soften it. But then I decided the hell with it. Lake had dominated the news since the debate. Now we were going to dominate it; "that would embarrass me" would put the press on him day and night. "What did he mean by that, Congressman Lake?" "Are you going to release your records in the next twenty-four hours?" "You've been in Congress three terms, but you've never released any medical records as yet. Why is that?"

I'd told everybody on the staff to play it coy when reporters called them. Never say it was Lake behind the drink plan, just say, "Anything's possible." Never say that Jim Lake had been treated for gonorrhea in the tenth year of his family-values marriage, only that we'd heard there was a shocking fact to be found in his medical records.

Even without Teresa pushing me, I'd known when I'd seen Lake's new commercial that I was going to tell Warren that we should go after him. No other choice. I'd overseen this kind of bombast twice. Once it had worked, once it hadn't. In the case of the former, a congressional opponent had managed to cover up a hit-and-run in a small town his father basically owned. In the case of the latter, the oppo people had come up with three counts of spousal abuse on a man who'd also managed to keep these off the official records. I knew this would be risky because he'd gone through AA five years ago and was now, by all accounts, including those of his wife, a very good husband. The electorate chose him over our man, who had a few problems of his own that the oppo folks on the other side had somehow missed.

We had pizza and beer as we watched the Chicago evening news. Three sets going so we didn't miss anything. We were slotted either story number one or story number two on each of them. And the leads all played heavily on the "suggestion" that Lake might have something to hide in his medical records. His press spokesman, a kid usually given to smirks, was somber and somewhat dazed when he faced the press, assuring them that Lake had nothing to hide and would address this question as soon as he returned to Chicago from Springfield later tonight. The kid, happily, looked miserable.

Only one station picked up on the inference that "anything's possible" might mean that Lake had had something to do with tampering with Warren's drink. "Asked for a clarification, the Nichols camp would say only that no accusations were being made, but that many possibilities were being considered both by them and by local police."

Beers were hoisted. Big, wet, beery kisses were exchanged. Teresa and Warren got so intense people started flickering the lights on and off to the great amusement of the lovers. For once the psychic rush was positive. We had reclaimed the argument. Somewhere lurked the information that Lake had been treated for gonorrhea while in the tenth year of his marriage. And the press was going to find it. And the press was going to ask him about it in the context of his constant criticism of our "libertine" society—single mothers, gay people, lurid TV shows, and, of course, the centerpiece of his attack, "those who would destroy the basis of our civilization, the sacred institution of marriage." You shouldn't be saying those things after requiring heavy doses of penicillin.

Somewhere along the line I got drunk and ended up making out with a thirty-seven-year-old nurse who worked as a volunteer. It was pure high school. By the time I thought I was going to get to third base in her nice warm Chevrolet, she had to go to the hospital, where she was on the night shift this week. She'd been drinking ginger ale.

One of the other volunteers gave me a ride to my hotel. I stopped at the desk and asked if anything had been left for me. The clerk, assessing my blood alcohol level, handed me a large manila envelope. In the elevator, I studied the reports that Tully had left for me. I'd spent two grand on nothing. He'd left a note inside saying that he'd actually worked two jobs for Wylie, the second relating to a painting of Wylie's stolen from a gallery he'd loaned it to. Wylie had hired Tully to follow two prominent fences. Not a damned thing to do with Warren being blackmailed.

I sprawled on the bed, not even bothering to take off my suit. It had been a long time since I'd had a beer drunk and it would have its revenge on me in the morning with a swollen head and dehydration.

Sometime in the process of falling into REM sleep, I realized that tomorrow night I was expected to drop off one million dollars . . .

CHAPTER 26

I took a cab to headquarters, then decided I'd best hit the café down the street first. I poured three cups of boiling coffee directly into my eyes. Faster that way. Soon now I'd be able to check off "human" in one of those little boxes where they ask the name of your species. It would be a proud moment for me and the entire clan.

I went to relieve myself and when I returned, Warren and one of his bodyguards were there. The guard was an ex-Marine. In his blue pin-striped suit and white shirt and tie he looked almost civilized. Now that Warren was big in the news again, he needed protection. The crazies would be coming out for sure now. Hopefully just the harmless crazies.

"Karl," Warren said politely, "would you mind sitting over there at the counter? I need to talk to Dev here privately."

"No problem, sir."

"He's the best of the best," Warren said as Karl left. "He has laser vision. You wouldn't believe what he sees that I miss every time."

Warren had a pol's love for celebrating people. It becomes an instinct after a certain number of years and a certain number of rubber-chicken dinners where you have to extol the virtues of a tubby little man who'd contributed X amount of dollars to the party for the past X number of years. Thank God there are such people, but by the time the speechwriter has had at them they sound as if they were a combination of astronaut, scholar, and clairvoyant.

"Guys like him are the reason we win wars, Dev."

"Yeah, except for the last two."

The smile was sour. "Never can let it lie, can you, Dev? Always have to spoil the moment."

"Guess I can only gag down so much bullshit, Warren. Sorry. Now let's talk about tonight."

This time the smile was coy. "Oh, I don't think we'll need much discussion."

"You have the money?"

"I have the money. Every penny of it."

"That's amazing." And it was. When R. D. Greaves was shaking us down, Warren had had to struggle to raise three hundred thousand. And now he had a million?

"I cashed some pretty heavy-duty bonds."

"I thought you couldn't do that."

"My CPA showed me a way to do it without attracting much attention."

"But I mean you said they were tied up and you couldn't get to them."

"A little white lie, Dev."

"Gee, you telling a lie. Who'da thunk it?"

"There you go again. Spoiling the moment."

I sipped some coffee. "I've never seen anybody this happy to be losing a million bucks."

"That's the thing. I'm not going to lose a million bucks."

"You're not?"

"No. And it'll be thanks to you. Because you're going to follow the money. You're going to wait in the shadows and see who makes the drop and then you're going to follow them."

"Ah."

"Just make sure you have your Glock. And make sure your car is all ready to go."

"This is just like TV."

"You see something wrong with it?"

"I see a lot wrong with it. Mainly that we have no way of verifying what's on the tape we get."

"We have to trust them."

"Nobody I trust more than a blackmailer."

"Then what the fuck is your idea, Dev, you sitting there so smug and everything?"

"I don't have a better idea, Warren."

Warren looked idiotically triumphant. The Hollywood smile was back in place. He'd kidded himself into believing—at least for a few giddy moments here—that everything was just hunky-dunky. "Things are going so well, Dev. Three different newspapers ran editorials this morning saying that Lake should release all his medical records."

"He respond yet?"

"Not yet. But we've got him boxed in. If he releases all his records, he's dead on the spot. And if he doesn't, we've got a club to beat him over the head with from now till Election Day. I just can't believe how this has turned around."

He was a kid again and that ten-speed he'd been wanting had just been wheeled up to his front porch and he was experiencing an orgasmic moment here.

It was all coming back to him—the power, the glamour, the glory of being a United States senator.

"You hit everything just right, Dev. And I really appreciate it."

"I'm going to spoil the moment again, Warren. We've still got two weeks to go. We don't know what their oppo people have on us. Fine to be happy but, man, don't take anything for granted."

His face crimped in distaste. He'd been junkie high and I was forcing him back to drab winter gray. "I'll do my best not to be happy, Dev. You know, I sure wouldn't want to piss you off by feeling better about the campaign."

"You're being stupid, Warren. All I said was—"

"All you said the other day was"—he leaned in—"that I was a piece of shit and you'd be glad to be rid of me. You think I've forgotten that, you're fucking crazy."

He stood up, signaling Karl. To me he said: "You'll have the briefcase about five this afternoon. I'd appreciate a call as to how it goes."

"Are we breaking up, Warren? You want your ring back?"

"The ladies think you're real cute. I don't. For what it's worth, I'd planned on firing your ass anyway, Dev."

A pretty good line to leave on.

Around two that afternoon Jim Lake's press person announced that all of the congressman's medical records would be released in twenty-four hours. That brought a lot of smiles from the staff. Kate seemed particularly amused: "Maybe he'll use the Latin word for gonorrhea. It sounds classier."

"There's no way he's releasing that," I said. "He's going to trick it up some way. The press already has a pretty good idea of what he's hiding and if it's not there, they're going to jump all over him."

"I could almost feel sorry for him," Laura said, "if he wasn't such a hater. That's what he's built his career on." She smiled and snapped her fingers. "There. I'm cured. I don't feel sorry for him at all." She addressed the rest of us. "Let's get together and tear his throat out."

We all went out for pizza and beer together. Even dour Gabe was enjoying himself. "I'm going to miss you people."

"God, if I didn't know better," Billy said, "I'd say Gabe is getting sentimental."

"I can't help it. I really like working with you people."

Kate said, "Well, we're going to miss *you* too, Gabe. We go back a long ways."

"Yes, and I've been a hail-fellow-well-met through every one of our times together. Always smiling. Always with something positive to say. Always there to make people glad that they're alive."

At first we all thought Gabe was being serious and had to wonder if he'd had some kind of mental breakdown in front of our eyes. Then he gave us his hippie grin and we all started laughing.

Back in the office, everybody drinking coffee to compensate for the two or three beers they'd had, I polled several of our key sites to see how the volunteers were doing getting out the message. You always expect some marginal exaggeration—"They are as the legions of Rome, Master!"—but even chopping the enthusiasm down twenty percent, it sounded as if the volunteers were working hard and taking on extra duties the closer the election drew.

Next I called three Chicago reporters I knew to see if they'd heard anything yet from Lake and his people. I didn't tell them the exact nature of what he was trying to hide, but I did say that it would be interesting if he claimed to be presenting his entire medical history. One of the reporters asked if she could "see all his records in case he doesn't come through. I'm assuming here, Dev, that *you* have them." "What a sordid accusation." "Yeah, right, babe."

Near the end of the afternoon Karl the bodyguard showed up with a stout black leather briefcase. It was padlocked. He handed me the key. "The senator said you'd know what this was."

"Thanks, Karl. Where's the senator now?"

"He's at the house in Evanston. He has the night off and he wants to relax."

"I appreciate you bringing this by."

He nodded as he surveyed the staff. "Nice to see people working this hard for the senator. We've got to make sure he wins."

Like most pols, Warren was most comfortable when he surrounded himself with true believers. They had their own doubts, of course, but they expressed them rarely if at all. Each entourage usually had one skeptic—in this case, me. But when the news got really bad, the rest of them stared at you as if your skepticism had caused nasty things to happen. And right after the campaign manager—almost always the first to get canned—you the consultant were next up. At the very latest you'd be fired the day after the election, win or lose. You had, merely by being honest with everyone, brought the campaign bad luck. You know, voodoo.

One by one people left for the day. All but Kate were headed back to the pizza place for more of the same. Kate said, "I'm going to bake a very special cake for my daughter tonight."

"Her birthday?"

"No, but I just feel like celebrating. That whole thing with the debate—seeing Warren that way . . ." She shrugged. "Past history." Then: "Oh, that report from the detective's been over here on the fax all day. I'm surprised nobody gave it to you."

The phone rang seconds after she left. It was Detective Sayers himself. "You get the report?"

"Haven't had time to look at it."

"Nothing special from what I can see. Thought you might look at how the crime scene broke down. Stuff we found."

"I'll bet you want to hear me say that I figured out who stiffed Warren's drink and who murdered Greaves."

"I thought you might have something. I sure don't."

A decent enough ploy—the sad, lonely cop who had nary a clue—but a bit broad to play believably to an old cynic like myself.

"Wish I could help you."

"I'll bet you do. Well, talk to you later."

"Thanks for the report."

"My pleasure."

Two minutes later the door opened. One of the older volunteers from up front escorted four high school journalists in. They wanted to interview me for their respective newspapers. I'd forgotten about it.

We spent nearly ninety minutes together and a lot of it was fun. They were bright kids for one thing and for another they had a serious interest in politics. I was surprised at the breadth of their knowledge. They knew just about every pol I mentioned in the course of citing various campaigns for this or that reason. And just at the end they focused on Congressman Lake and why he seemed reluctant—even a bit afraid—of releasing his health records.

"I'm afraid I can't give you the answer. He's the only one who'd know that. What I can tell you is that after the debate where Senator Nichols got so sick, Lake made a big deal of the senator's health. He forced us to respond the way we did. By making our entire medical history available online."

"Is Congressman Lake in trouble if he *doesn't* release his records?"

"Hard to say. The press and the public will decide that." I said this having no doubt that the press now stood ready to bring him down.

The volunteer came back and told the students that their time was up. It had been an enjoyable break.

I grabbed the briefcase Karl had delivered from under my desk and then filled my own briefcase with two different field reports I planned to study later tonight. Then I grabbed the police report about the crime scene and gave it a quick look. The door to the dressing room hadn't been jimmied; there was no evidence that anything had been damaged inside. That pretty much confirmed that one of the staffers had put the drug in Warren's drink.

I'd shut the phone off while the students were here. Now I checked for messages. Only one. My friend in the police department said that the medical examiner was still trying to determine if Greaves's death had been a crime or an accident.

I shut off the lights, taking note of how badly my right hand was trembling.

CHAPTER 27

There was a conventioneers' dance in the main ballroom of the hotel. I'd parked my car per instructions from the blackmailer, then come inside and suddenly it was 1943. I was about to say "Nineteen forty-three again." But there was no *again* for me, of course. I hadn't come along till much later. But I'd developed a real passion for music of that era, especially the female singers, Billie Holiday and Jo Stafford and Lena Horne in particular.

So I stood near the back entrance of the place, ten minutes early, watching for signs of anybody sneaking up on my car, which was parked in the front row. My plan was to make a run for him, grabbing tape and blackmailer alike. I had my Glock, brass knuckles, and a small billy. I was ready for a war. I hated to admit that I was looking forward to it. But I realized that it would free me of my lingering depression. There's something to be said for simply taking action, a kind of purgative that doesn't do our species proud.

I had to step aside several times to let people in and out of the back door. I was in the middle of letting someone out when I saw a dark shape emerge from a six-deep row of cars and begin working its way slowly toward mine. The way it kept looking right to left, the way it hunched down slightly, the way it kept patting its gloved hand against its chest—was that where the tape was being kept?—made its purpose clear.

I got ready to move. I pushed the door open and stepped out into the dark night. The mercury vapor lights cast a strange color over all the new sports cars and Benzes and the handful of Rolls-Royces. The figure was very close to my car now.

I kept to the shadows. A narrow sidewalk stretched to the parking lot. Walls were close in on both sides. But there was enough space that I could stand on a strip of grass and watch it.

And then it stood straight up, a grandmotherly sort who clutched her purse to her chest as if she feared an imminent mugging. You get a lot of false leads in this business.

I wasn't paying any attention to the small groups of people who came out to get their cars. They were all dressed very well, all seeming liquor happy and Black Card confident, headed to their cars and the prospect of hitting some of the tonier nightspots in the city.

So I didn't even consider that I was in danger until he brought something heavy down against the back of my skull. Not once but twice. He wanted me out. I was conscious long enough to get a mental still photo of what happened next. I fell sideways, onto the sidewalk. I hit it in such a way that my nose cut against the edge of the walk and sent a splash of blood into the air and right onto a gray trouser leg. My last thought being that there was something familiar about the material and pattern of that trouser leg—

. . .

I was aware of pain just before I opened my eyes. The picture presented was of an acoustically tiled ceiling with a square of electric light filtered through a horizontally patterned piece of plastic.

A woman said: "He's coming around. I'd appreciate some fresh water here."

She pushed her pleasing face into my view. "I'm Dr. Ryan. I'm a guest here and they asked me to help. Can you remember what happened to you?"

No memory problems. "Somebody knocked me out." I'd been shaken enough by the attack to want to say more. But I had to be careful and give no hint of what was behind the attack.

"You were found on the north sidewalk that leads to the parking lot."

"Yes, I was going out to my car."

"And somebody just hit you?" A male voice. Man in suit. Detective. Unmistakable.

"Probably a mugger."

"Didn't look that way to me. Your clothes weren't torn. You still had your wallet with several hundred-dollar bills. You've got your watch, which is expensive, and your cell phone. I don't think a mugger would leave you with all those things."

"Would you help me sit up, Doctor?"

It was a long trip to rest on my bottom. But once there I found that the pain subsided considerably. "How long have I been out?"

Dr. Ryan was a middle-aged woman with very soft blue eyes and a remarkably erotic mouth. She wore a blue cocktail dress cut just low enough to show the top of her freckled cleavage. The detective, who'd yet to give his name, was burly, surly, and suspicious.

"Do I need any stitches?"

The doctor was about to speak. The detective spoke first, over her. "No stitches, no concussion from what the doctor can see. The only blood was from your nose. We estimate that you weren't on that sidewalk unconscious very long, because of the heavy foot traffic. Somebody saw you and cell-phoned the front desk. You've been here about ten minutes. The doctor doesn't think you need an ambulance. I asked her to let me ask you a few questions. Does that catch us up to date to your satisfaction?"

The last question was sarcastic enough to bring a frown to the doctor's wonderful mouth. "I'm not quite sure why you're treating him this way, Detective Slattery, and I have to say I don't like it. Somebody knocked him out. He doesn't know who and he doesn't know why. That seems reasonable."

"Well, it sure wasn't any mugger who knocked him out. Otherwise they'd have taken everything he had on him."

My head was able to glance around the white room without undue pain. This was a real infirmary. I was on a comfortable examination table. The walls were lined with sparkling white glass-fronted cases filled with medicines and medical equipment of all kinds. No wonder I liked this hotel so much.

Dr. Ryan ignored him. "The only problem we had—and it wasn't that much of a problem—was getting your nosebleed to stop. You got very little on you but the sidewalk is a mess. There's no sign that you broke it or damaged it in any way. But the best course would be to send you to the ER, where they can X-ray your head and nose as well. That's what I'd do if I were you. You could rest here for a while and then drive yourself to the hospital—it's right nearby—or I could call for an ambulance."

Slattery moved in. "We'll need you to sign a statement."

"It won't be much of a statement. It's what I told you. I was walking to my car when somebody hit me from behind."

"And you can't think of any enemy you might have who'd do something like that?"

"I'm a political consultant. We don't usually resort to violence."

"Political consultant? Who's your man?"

"Nichols."

"Figures. I'm a Lake man myself."

I smiled at Dr. Ryan. "Why doesn't that surprise me?"

"What's that supposed to mean?"

I was irritable from everything that had happened in the last twenty minutes. I said, "You've been riding my ass since I came to. You think there was some personal reason I was attacked. I don't. I can't rule it out, but I also can't think of anybody who'd do it. I've basically given you my statement twice. I was walking out to my car and somebody hit me from behind and knocked me to the sidewalk. That's all I know and that's the sum and substance of my statement. And I don't have anything to add. And I don't plan on changing it one bit. So if you want me to stop down tomorrow morning and sign it, I'll be happy to. How's that?"

Amusement played in the gentle blue eyes of the good doctor. "For now, I want to turn the light off and let our patient here rest up a little. If that's all right with you, Detective Slattery?"

He growled something I didn't understand, nodded to Dr. Ryan, and left.

"Everywhere I go I make new friends."

A pleasing smile. "You're sensitive to what others think of you, I see. I guess I got a slightly different sense of the detective than you did."

"He was just embarrassed by how much he admires me."

"So that's it." She pointed to the door. "I'll be out there for another half hour. I need to check messages and call a few hospitals. As I said, you can rest here or go to an ER."

"Or do whatever I like?"

"Or do whatever you like with the understanding that I'd prefer you go to the ER and have a couple of X rays."

"So it's my responsibility."

"Yes, it is. It's your responsibility."

"Then I guess I'll go wash up and probably go upstairs to my room. By the way, shouldn't you be at the dance?"

"I would've escaped even if you hadn't had your problem. This is the awards part and it really gets dull."

"I won't tell them you said that."

"Just be careful. Remember that."

Ten minutes later I was in my room, washing up and changing clothes. The suit I'd been wearing was muddy in a few places and torn in one, under the arm. There were blood spatters on my right pants leg.

And then I remembered the gray pants leg that had been the last image I'd had before slipping into unconsciousness. Now that I was fully awake I recognized why the particular gray color and weave of the trouser leg had looked so familiar. It belonged to the uniform that the bellhops wore here. Red blazers, gray trousers. A bellhop had attacked me.

I wore a white crewneck sweater and jeans with a leather jacket and hiking boots. I figured I might be having some trouble tonight. I might as well dress for it. The Glock completed my attire for the evening.

The lobby was still crowded. The restaurant had a line of people waiting to get in and both lounges sounded full to overflowing. Either that or they had a handful of the noisiest drunks this side of the Mississippi River.

I started checking for the bellhop. There were four on duty at this hour. I was assuming that the blood would be easy to spot on his trouser leg. But the longer I looked, the more clearly I realized that as I was slipping away I was apt to see things that might not be there— yes, there'd been a lot of blood given the condition of my nose—but no, this didn't necessarily mean that he'd gotten any on him. The other possibility was that yes, he'd gotten blood on his trouser leg but he had a spare pair of trousers in his locker and had already changed.

I sat with a paperback in a chair next to the glass elevator that worked nonstop. The most exclusive section of the hotel was the restaurant on the top floor. I'd looked at the prices. Only a lobbyist could afford them.

Who knew that I'd turn out to be the guy in all those TV private-eye shows who sat in the lobby pretending to read while actually scanning the people to find the guilty person? Well, we all had our spot in life.

He showed up about fifteen minutes into my stakeout. He got off one of the regular elevators and walked to the front desk. Even from here I could see spatters of something on his trouser leg. He was young, no more than twenty-five, with a headful of curly blond hair and an insolent smile. He was the guy who could fix you up with ladies, get you smack, even find you a cockfight to attend. You could see him on the cover of *Pimp Monthly* as "Our Man of the Year."

I didn't know where he was going and I didn't care. I followed him. He didn't become aware of me until he was in a narrow corridor. He suddenly started looking over his shoulder. But he was too late. In three steps I was right behind him, in four I had a handful of his hair, smashed his face into the wall, and gave him a kidney punch that stood him up straight and then folded him in half. His face was bloody from the wall slam. I grabbed his hair again and dragged him outside, where I stood him up straight again so I could give my knee a good target for his crotch. He instinctively tried to double up and grab his wounded area, but I wasn't going to give him any indulgences. I threw him up against the wall and said, "Who hired you?"

His wild, frightened eyes grew even more frightened. He gaped around, trying to find some way of escape. But there wasn't any escape possible.

"I want to know who hired you. If you don't tell me in thirty seconds I start working on your ribs. You understand?"

The night. Planes circling O'Hare. Giant trucks racing through the darkness. The dance music from inside the ballroom. The smells of fresh chilled air out here, and the stench of the bellhop having wet himself.

I hit him hard and square in the stomach. Blood began oozing from the corner of his mouth. His eyes told of defeat and shame. He said, the blood making it difficult to speak, "Just had a phone number. Never met her."

"Her? You must've gotten her name?"

He shook his head. "No. Honest. I never got her name."

He painfully explained the situation, grimacing every time one of his body parts sent a pain message to his brain. He'd been contacted by phone by a woman who told him that she wanted him to pick up a briefcase for her. She told him what the car looked like and what I looked like. She also told him that I would undoubtedly be watching from the sidewalk and that he was to come up behind me and knock me out. Nothing that would inflict serious damage. Just take me out for five to ten minutes. And so he had.

"But if I hit you too hard, I'm sorry."

"You got the briefcase?"

He nodded. "It's in my locker."

"You open it?"

"She told me not to."

"How are you supposed to get it to her?"

"I'm meeting her out in the parking lot in fifteen minutes. I give her the briefcase and she gives me a thousand dollars in hundreds." He was getting much better at speaking with a mouthful of blood.

"Let's go get the briefcase."

"What?"

"You said you've got the briefcase in your locker. We're going to go get it. You and I. Then we're going to wait in the parking lot for her to show up."

"I really need that thousand dollars, dude."

He must have been feeling much stronger now. Calling somebody "dude" requires a certain amount of energy.

"We'll make a trade. You lose your thousand dollars and I don't turn you over to the cops. How's that?"

He seemed to think about it, which suggested that he was a harder case than I'd guessed. I'd trade a thousand dollars to stay out of Cook County Jail for six months—his likely sentence—but he wanted that grand badly enough to actually consider risking life in a cell for a thousand dollars.

"Shit," he said.

"What's your name, by the way?"

"Tim Gaines."

I took my hands from the bunched shirt I had pressed against his collarbone.

"I can't afford no police record. They'd fire my ass here for sure. Insurance won't cover hops if they've got a police record."

"Sounds reasonable. Now let's go get that briefcase."

"I told my girlfriend we were going to Vegas on that money. I already had another fifteen hundred saved to put with it."

"C'mon. Let's go get the briefcase."

Even in the newest hotel there are sections below that remind you of the catacombs. We went down two levels to a sub-subbasement, the effect unpleasant for a claustrophobe like me. I could smell the heat from the laundry and hear the boom and grind of different motors at work. The men's locker room had a shower area and different kinds of aftershave. Picking up the briefcase was anticlimactic.

Back upstairs, we went outside. He took up a position at the curb as I'd instructed. I wanted the arriving car to be as close to me as possible. I'd wait until the vehicle pulled up and he'd started to approach it. Then I'd appear, run around the car to the driver's side, and show the Glock. If the driver tried to pull away I'd shoot out the two tires on my side.

Gaines kept looking back at me. His nervousness started to make me anxious, too. All this had to be done quickly. Twice he walked off the curb, giving me the impression that he saw the car pulling up. But both times were false alarms. My armpits were soaked with sweat. Despite the cold I was in need of changing shirts.

Finally he made his move and it was the right one. A two-year-old Pontiac sedan pulled up and he immediately started walking toward it.

I let him reach the car and start talking to the driver before I sprinted out from the shadows and ducked down as I worked my way around the rear of the car and up to the driver's window.

I already knew who I'd see. I'd ridden in this car many times during the campaign.

While she talked to him, I tapped on her window with my Glock. She turned to face me, looking alternately shocked, angry, and then hurt, as if I'd betrayed her in some way.

I opened the door and said, "Slide over, Laura. I'm driving."

CHAPTER | 28

"Where are you taking me?"

"We're going to drive around and you're going to tell me what the fuck is going on here."

"I don't want to tell you anything, Dev. And I don't have to."

"We could always go right to the police."

"That's bullshit and you know it. They'd want to see the tape. And it would all be over for Nichols."

"What the hell is this all about? Why did you pay Greaves to make that tape?"

"I already told you I don't want to say anything. I'll only talk to my lawyer, nobody else."

"What the hell has Warren ever done to you?"

"He fired Wylie. And Phil never recovered. He'd been sober for six years but he started drinking again." Pause. "I want to call my lawyer."

"Be my guest. Use your cell. Call him. I'll drive you over there and wait till you're finished."

"And then what?"

"Then I want you to tell me what this is all about. I think you owe the campaign that much."

"I don't owe the campaign anything."

"What were you planning to do with the tape?"

"Send it to Jim Lake."

"Great. That's loyalty."

"Yeah, Dev. The same kind of loyalty he showed to Phil."

"Phil, Phil, Phil. I don't get the connection here."

"The connection was that I was in love with him."

"Oh."

"Even though he wasn't in love with me. He saw me the way he would a sister. We even slept together but it didn't help him."

"Help him in what way?"

"Help him get over this other woman."

"Anybody I know?"

"I'm calling David. You need to be quiet."

The call didn't last much more than a minute. He was awake, and no, it wasn't too late. He'd put on some coffee for her. She knew the address. It was not far from Loyola University, a genteel two-story brick home with white shutters and a screened-in porch running the length of the front. I parked in the driveway and cut the lights.

"You're just going to sit here?"

"I'm just going to sit here."

"There's no guarantee I'm going to tell you anything."

"I realize that."

"You could always take a cab back to your hotel."

"And miss all the fun of sitting out here?"

"You don't have any right to do this."

"You know the worst thing about this is that you're a stranger. I'm serious. I don't know who you are. You're this beautiful young woman and that part hasn't changed. But everything else has. Especially your voice. I've never heard this kind of anger and hatred in your voice before. And the way you look at me. I don't know what I've ever done to you that would make you hate me, too."

"You took Phil's place."

"But I didn't fire him, Laura. I only came on because there was a vacancy."

"Maybe I'm being irrational about you. But I'm not being irrational about Warren."

"I'm quitting the day after the election. Win or lose."

"What? Are you serious?"

"Very serious. I don't hold Warren in any higher regard than you do. I'm sick of him and all his lies."

"Well, then I owe you an apology."

"You can make it up to me by telling me what's going on."

"I'll see what my lawyer says."

She started to turn toward her door, but I grabbed her wrist. "One more question."

"Let go of me, Dev."

"Did you kill Greaves?"

"Are you fucking insane, Dev? Do you think I go around killing people?"

I let go of her wrist.

And with that she was gone. The dome light flashed bright for a moment as she got out of the car. A glimpse of that lovely face, so troubled now.

She stayed for slightly more than ninety minutes. I listened to talk shows dealing with the coming election. The vampires were out, sucking the blood from any serious discussion with wild claims and accusations. Most of the cranks hated Warren. He was described variously as a socialist, a communist, a supporter of terrorism, a sissy, and a despiser of all that was good and true in this great land of ours. Lake, on the other hand, was described as a man we could count on when the

Martians attacked. Or the Venusians. I couldn't quite figure out which alien nation they had in mind.

Harsh wind sure made the lemony glow of the downstairs windows look awful cozy. Watching a late movie with a woman I was in love with, a drink or two, and then some comfortable sex before we fell asleep. All things possible. That would be my first priority after I walked away from Warren's camp. Finding a woman. I was ready to resort to sandwich boards if need be. And on Michigan Avenue. In broad daylight.

She was a bit drunk when she came back to the car. And she had the hiccups to prove it.

"Everything's going to hell," she said. "I'll probably be in prison a month from now. The thing I worry about most"—pause for a hiccup—"is my parents. I was the first person to graduate from college in my family. The Chinese"—pause for hiccup—"are proud people. Though sometimes you wouldn't know it. All that bowing and"—pause for hiccup—"crap."

"You fixed up Warren's drink, too?"

"Yeah. It was actually"—pause—"easy."

I drove slowly back to the hotel, listening to her tell me, between hiccups, what had transpired inside with her lawyer. He had told her that it was unlikely that Warren would bring the matter of taping him or extortion to the police given the nature of the tape. The police would assure him that the contents of the tape would forever be held in secret, but in this age of the media, "secret" was anything that lasted for more than forty-eight hours. But she was convinced that she was headed for prison despite all his reassurances, even when the lawyer said Warren couldn't even go after her for the stiffed drink. He'd be worried that that too would lead somehow to the tape.

"So where is the tape now?" I said.

"Right"—pause for hiccup—"here."

And with that she reached in her purse and brought forth this year's version of the Maltese Falcon. The McGuffin. The one thing everybody wanted. She held it up, streetlights and traffic lights and bistro lights flashing behind it as we moved down the city streets.

That tape should have glowed or been encrusted with barnacles or been heavy with the scrawl of some ancient and mysterious language. But it was just a standard miniature videocassette of the kind you can get at the supermarket for a buck or two.

"Are you sure there aren't any other copies floating around?"

"I made sure of that." And without a single hiccup. "The only time the tape was out of my hands was when I let Greaves use it for a few minutes to show you. I was in the other room listening. Then what I wanted was his laptop. I trashed his daughter's place looking for it but I didn't have any luck."

I decided against telling her that I had it. That might come later.

She explained to me that she'd been with Greaves the morning they'd taped Warren, never let Greaves out of her sight in case he had the idea of making a copy for himself. She had the one and only copy.

"So when he said he had the original tape, he was lying to me?"

"Ab"—pause for hiccup—"solutely."

She laid the tape on the seat between us. "All yours."

"Thank you."

A chortle. "Now *you* should blackmail the bastard."

"I just want to get away from him. Fast as I can."

"I'm with you on that."

"I'm curious. What were you going to do with a million dollars?"

She held up the briefcase and patted it. "Give it to Kate."

"Kate? She makes good money and she comes from money."

"Her dad died a while back and her brother took over the estate. I don't know if you ever met him." Pause for hiccup. "He's a know-it-all. He lost nearly everything for them. They're not poor, but they aren't rich anymore"—pause for hiccup—"either."

"Why would Kate need a million dollars?"

"Because Warren won't give her very much for their daughter."

"Their daughter? Warren's the father of Kate's daughter?"

She nodded. And then, in between hiccups, she told me the rest. Phil Wylie had long been in love with Kate. But Kate had long been in love with Warren. The falling-out between Phil and Warren had been over Kate. Phil felt that Warren should pay an informal kind of child support. Warren felt that Kate was a "big girl" and had known the consequences of having an affair with a married man. He gave her a small "stipend" every month. But he wouldn't acknowledge paternity. Kate could have gone public but didn't because she held out hope that someday Warren would leave Teresa and marry her. This was what Phil and Warren had clashed about. Phil thought Warren was acting despicably. Warren said that Phil was being irrational. Phil resigned in a great rage. Laura watched as he declined into paranoia and helplessness, ending in suicide.

"Then nobody murdered him?"

"No," she said. "I was making us dinner in the kitchen when he jumped. I panicked and got out of there as fast as I could."

I saw a Denny's and swerved in there.

"You're going into a Denny's? Do you have any idea what kind of civil rights record they have?"

"You need coffee and so do I. I've got to think all this through."

"Denny's," she said. Hiccup. "They'll probably throw me out because I'm Chinese."

CHAPTER | *29*

✶ ✶ ✶ ✶ I exercised in the hotel gym the next morning and
✶ ✶ ✶ then had room service bring me up a poached egg
✶ ✶ ✶ ✶ and a slice of toast and a pot of coffee. After the food
✶ ✶ ✶ and a shower, I called Warren.

"Where are you now?"

"I just visited three plant gates. Why?"

"I want you to come up to my hotel room."

"We finally going to have sex, are we?"

"Nobody else. Alone."

"I was hoping for a three-way."

"When can I expect you?"

"You sound pissed."

"When can I expect you?"

"You're taking over, huh? How about half an hour?"

"I'll see you then."

While I waited for him, I called my daughter and asked her how
she'd like to see me for a few days. She was just as excited as I'd hoped

she'd be. I sure was excited. Then I got on my computer and arranged for a round-trip plane ticket four days hence.

Warren arrived five minutes early.

He wore his tan camel's-hair overcoat, one of his best blue suits, a white shirt with the golden collar bar, and his favorite blue rep tie. He put on some swagger to back up his first words to me: "I don't like being pushed around by somebody on my payroll."

"Tough shit, Warren. And you won't have to worry about taking any more shit from me. I'm resigning here and now."

"What?"

"There's coffee on that table over there. There's also a videotape. *The* videotape. I've been assured that that's the only copy."

"Are you kidding me?"

"Sure, Warren. This is all a gag. All the shit I've been through, I did it just for fun."

"My God," he said, slipping out of his overcoat and draping it on a leather chair.

He sat down and picked up the tape. He held it up as if he could see it simply by staring at the black plastic encasement. "I don't believe this. So they fell for it, huh?"

"You mean the way you shortchanged them by eight hundred thousand? No, they knew about it right away." Laura and I checked the briefcase just before I let her out of the car. Good old Warren had cheated again.

I sat across from him at the table.

"God, Dev. I really appreciate this. All that bullshit is behind us now. That is if they were telling you the truth about this being the only copy."

"I'm positive it is."

"How the hell did you pull it off?"

"It doesn't matter. You have the tape. They have your two hundred thousand."

He leaned back. The pleasure in his gaze was replaced by suspicion. "You keep saying 'they.' Who are we talking about here exactly, anyway?"

"I have no idea."

"What?"

"Something went wrong on their end. A falling-out. Or somebody just got scared. We did everything by telephone. The guy I talked to said he just wanted it to be over. He was obviously an amateur. He was also very nervous. He brought up the subject of copies of the tape. He explained that there was only one copy, because if there were others floating around the police could trace them back to him. That's why I think they or whoever just got terrified of getting caught. A pro would never have accepted the two hundred thousand. If his motive was political, he would have turned it over to a TV station. If it was just money, he would've added on another quarter million just because you screwed him. But like I said, this guy was no pro."

Still suspicious: "He have anything to do with queering my drink?"

"He said he did it and that it wasn't difficult."

After a long pause, he said, "You're not telling me the truth here, Dev. Something's wrong with your story."

There was a lot wrong with my story, but I didn't want to involve Laura. If she was to be found out, he'd have to do the finding himself.

"Accept your good fortune, Warren."

"So you're going to leave it like that?"

"Just like that."

"I want the truth."

"You've got the truth as far as you need to know it. Now take the tape and get the hell out of here."

"The cops could make you talk."

I enjoyed laughing at him. "Think about it, Warren. You sic the cops on me and the tape story'll be front and center. You really want that?"

"You don't have the right to do this."

"Sure I do. Now get up and get out."

I walked around to the side of his chair and said, "Let's go, Warren. I've got things to do today." I was burning to tell him that I knew about Kate's child, but I was afraid that if I did he'd know I'd learned about it from Laura.

He stood up and did a very stupid thing. He swung on me. He was a better puncher than I'd thought. He didn't hit me square in the face, but his punch landed hard enough on my ear to induce great momentary pain. He was getting ready to throw another one but I was quicker. I hit him right below the sternum, hit him hard enough to drive him back a few feet. I not only took his breath, I brought him to nausea. He covered his mouth and stumbled toward the bathroom. Even senators sound disgusting when they're puking. He stayed in there for a while washing up.

When he came out, I was holding his overcoat in one hand and his tape in the other. He angrily swiped the tape from me and shoved it in the pocket of the overcoat, which he took with his other hand. Then he walked straight to the door and out without once looking back. He closed the door gently behind him.

I wished I'd been able to beat him up, but he had a campaign to run. Black eyes and a broken nose are a bitch to explain.

CHAPTER 30

A campaign luncheon was scheduled for Warren, sponsored by a civic group famous for the food it served. Gabe, Kate, Laura, and Billy would be there. So it would be a good time to sneak into the office, get my stuff, and sneak back out.

I sat drinking coffee in the hotel restaurant, waiting for noon and allowing myself a few moments of orgasmic self-pity.

Gosh, and here we had Mrs. Conrad's little boy Dev, always trying to make this a better world, getting stomped on for all his troubles. What a decent, righteous hero-type he was. And such a giving man, too. The perfect husband, the perfect father. If only those around him could see past his cynicism and pain and recognize him for the gallant man he really was.

But I couldn't kid myself very long. I was just as dirty as the rest of them. I pretended otherwise. I needed to or I couldn't do my job. I had to try and function as a conscience of sorts. But what kind of conscience was I? I was doing everything I could to destroy Jim

Lake. I believed he would continue to perpetuate the lies and constitutional perversions of the current administration. I believed that he would continue to use the real threat of terrorism for nothing more than political gain. This crew couldn't stick up a gas station let alone win a war.

But vile as Lake was, I was just as vile. I was going to use his one-time venereal disease to bring him down. I fought his fight on his terms and had no regrets. And if Warren was a deceitful, arrogant peacock, so be it. All these stories we're taught about George Washington and Abraham Lincoln. They make me cringe with their sentimental bullshit. Most great leaders are deeply flawed men. George Washington mightily abused his open-ended expense account during his first term. But it's what they do for the common good that matters. So we put up with them because in general they're no better or no worse than the rest of us.

My trouble with Warren now was that he wouldn't do right by Kate and that he'd helped destroy a decent but troubled friend named Phil Wylie. Warren's flaws weren't all that exotic, but I cared deeply about Kate and had come to admire Phil Wylie in the days since his death.

I spent twenty minutes in my office filling up a small cardboard box with goodies I probably wouldn't be needing to look at ever again. The last things I took down were the eight hardcover books I kept on a shelf above my computer. Novels by Fitzgerald, Nathanael West, Raymond Chandler, Doctorow, Theodore Dreiser, David Madden, Joyce Carol Oates, and Richard Matheson. I read them when I needed to zone out of here, desperate to remind myself that there were other and equally important worlds.

Only after I dealt with the books did I take a closer look at the notes on my desk. There were three of them, from Gabe, Laura, and Kate respectively. Kate had also left me the two-week expense breakdown, which, for some reason, I started looking through. No reason to, now that I was no longer associated with Warren. I suppose it was just habit. Seeing if we were anywhere near our goal of containing costs.

The report ran to three pages with airline charges listed last. One line stood out. A round-trip ticket had been purchased, but the ticket holder had canceled before the flight.

The round-trip had been to Galesburg, Illinois. The trip I'd sent Billy on. The trip he'd written a very persuasive field report about.

Apparently without ever having gone there.

I wanted to check that date against another piece of information. I hadn't closed my computer up yet. I logged on and went through several days of *Tribune* headlines until I came to the story I wanted.

On the same morning Billy had canceled his flight, R. D. Greaves had been found dead in his hotel apartment.

I was shrugging into my coat when the phone rang.

"I'm calling on my cell, Bunny. I'm in the ladies' room. This luncheon is really dull." Kate. Trying hard to sound happy. But not succeeding. "What are you up to?"

"Just packing things up."

"You make that sound so final."

"Just for the weekend." I wasn't ready to tell her the truth, that I was leaving the campaign. I had other things I needed to do first. "You okay?"

"Pretty much."

"That's not real convincing."

Long silence. "I guess I might as well tell you."

I was half-afraid to hear. "You're unhappy. I'd appreciate knowing why. Maybe I can help."

"Not with this, Bunny. Teresa found out that Warren and I once had a little thing."

No mention of the baby.

"Enterprising lady. Hired a hacker. Went through our e-mails."

"E-mails are dangerous."

"But it was very civilized, actually. She came over to my place and told me she'd found out. What she wanted was for me to tell her that it was over. That now we just worked together, Warren and I."

"That must have been some conversation."

"I left a message on your room machine. I just needed to hear your voice."

"You think things are cool now?"

"She doesn't want any publicity. She wants to go back to Washington and pick right up where she left off. And I sure don't want any publicity. Wouldn't want anything of this to touch on my sweet little daughter."

"Your daughter's all that matters."

"What's so funny is that I don't give a damn about Warren anymore and neither does she. We were both laughing about that. All she's worried about is that the scandal might hurt him politically and that would hurt her in getting back to Washington."

"Good old Warren."

"Well, I need to get back to that boring luncheon. Bye, Bunny."

CHAPTER 31

I was on autopilot for the next forty-five minutes. I'd parked my car next to the side door, so loading my stuff into it was no problem. And then I started driving. But even if I wasn't aware of it, I had a destination. I kept on driving.

I sat in the car for a long time and just stared at the second-floor apartment. Maybe I should forget it. Just go back to my hotel. You could make a case that he'd done the world a favor. There were too many R. D. Greaveses in the world anyway.

He wouldn't have done it without a good reason. Killing wouldn't have come naturally to him. He would have been pushed into it. That I was certain of.

But then my fear for him became fear for the campaign. I was still a political operative. The implications of all this started scaring me.

Which would be worse? The public knowing that family-values Jim Lake had been unfaithful to his wife and picked up VD because of it?

Or that Senator Nichols had employed a staffer who was implicated in a murder?

But the operative in me was working fast.

How about the family-values man with VD who'd employed R. D. Greaves? Maybe dragging Greaves's history into it would be enough.

I knocked. Inside I could hear the TV. Billy answered the door.

"I thought I'd stop by and see if we owe you any expense money for that Galesburg trip. You didn't hand any chits in. And why aren't you at that luncheon?"

"I'm feeling under the weather, Dev. I didn't go in to work today."

"I need to talk to you, Billy. I need for you to tell me where you were when you were supposed to be in Galesburg." The screen door was locked inside. I rattled the knob. "Open up, Billy."

"Come back tomorrow."

"Open the door, Billy."

"You don't have any right—"

I looked straight at him through the rusted screening. "Sure I do, Billy. Sure I do."

He shook his head. Sighed. But he opened the door.

The first thing he did was shut off the TV. The second thing he did was pour more whiskey from the bottle on the coffee table into his glass. The third thing he did was say, "I filed a report, didn't I? So I had to have been there, right?"

"You forgot one thing. Your canceled plane ticket. It showed up on the printout from the airline."

"Story of my life."

"Oh, bullshit, Billy. It's not the story of your life. You're a very hot speechwriter. You just made a mistake. You made the mistake most of us would."

"You wouldn't have made that mistake."

"Are you crazy? Of course I would've. And so would Warren and

Gabe. Laura and Kate, they probably wouldn't have, because they're smarter than we are."

A brief smile. "That's for sure." Then, "You want a drink?"

"No, thanks, Billy."

I sat down. The apartment was comfortably warm and smelled of freshly made popcorn. And real butter. Put that quality of popcorn together with a good movie and you had a decent time for human beings, lonely or otherwise.

He'd already finished the drink he'd just poured for himself. He was now pouring another one.

"So what did you do to Greaves?"

"I don't know what you're talking about, Dev." But his voice was shaky and he'd taken to blinking for no apparent reason. "We went to a movie."

"Who went to a movie?"

"Beth and I."

"Oh?"

"Yes, we went to a movie and then we went and got a pizza and that was when the news came on the TV about R.D."

"I see. So it was a complete surprise then?"

"I'm not a killer."

"I know you're not, Billy. And I'm not accusing you of being one. What I'm describing here was accidental. Unintentional. Remember, the police said that was a possibility, too."

"That's just about the way it happened, too."

Beth came into the living room from the kitchen. You expect people involved in a death to pull a Joan Crawford. You know, a big melodramatic snit ending in cries of "Yes, I did it and I'm glad I did!"

What you don't expect is a pretty young woman nibbling popcorn out of an enormous blue plastic bowl to come ambling in and say what Beth had just said.

That's just about the way it happened, too.

She went over and sat on the arm of the sofa and said, "You want some popcorn, Dev? I can get you a bowl if you like."

"No, thanks. Why don't you finish what you were saying? You said that I was pretty much right, the way I scoped it out."

A shrug of her thin shoulders. "He found out I went to a lawyer."

"I'm not following."

Billy said, "The way her mother died. The cops always felt that R.D. killed her by pushing her down those stairs, but they could never prove it."

"But I wouldn't let it go. And two days ago I got the woman who lives in the apartment above where R.D. and my mom lived—Mrs. Neely—to admit she heard my mom screaming for help. Right after that she heard somebody falling down the stairs."

"Why didn't she tell this to the police?"

"Scared. Turns out R.D. threatened her. Told her he'd kill her if she said anything to me or the police."

"So she agreed to talk to you after R.D. was dead."

She nodded. Extracted a dainty amount of popcorn from the big blue bowl.

"You said you went to a lawyer."

"Umm-hmmm." Chewing popcorn and then swallowing it. "And my lawyer drinks where R.D.'s lawyer does and made the mistake of telling R.D.'s lawyer that I'd been to see him."

"So that when you went to see R.D. he blew up."

"And came at me with the fireplace poker. I was able to duck, but then he grabbed me by the throat. And that's when I kicked him on the shin. I got free. He lunged at me, but he couldn't get his balance and tripped right into the stone edge of the thing. I called 911 right away and got out of there. Then I called Billy. He canceled his trip to Galesburg. He knew how crazy I was over what'd happened."

The dispassion told me how little she'd ultimately thought of him.

234

I suppose when Mrs. Neely confirmed for her the fact that R.D. had actually killed her mother, not even Beth could feel a sentimental attachment to him any longer. Suspecting is one thing. Knowing for sure is another.

"I wanted to take the blame," Billy said. He must have been feeling better. He reached over and she pushed the big blue bowl in his direction. Billy's hand was so full of popcorn, some of it was tumbling from his closed fist.

"First thing, Beth," I said. "Get a different lawyer. In fact, let *me* get you a lawyer."

"It did piss me off that he told R.D.'s lawyer."

"Second, I want to ask you a favor."

She seemed perplexed. "Sure. I mean, I guess. What is it?"

"The other night I asked you about a videotape. Did you ever find out anything about it?"

"No, why?"

"I want you to forget I ever asked you that question."

"Hell, Dev, what are you talking about?" Billy said.

I smiled. "I'm not talking about anything. I didn't ask you that question the other night and I'm not asking you that question today."

The confusion remained on Beth's face for a few more seconds and then she seemed to understand what was really going on here. "I see." She was angry.

"You see?"

"I always told Billy you were a real asshole and maybe now he'll agree with me. You're going to get me a lawyer—your lawyer—so he or she can make sure I don't mention the videotape to the police."

"We really need to win this campaign," I said.

"I hate Lake as much as you do." She glanced at me and then at Billy and then back to me. "I could go to prison here, but you don't give a damn. All you care about is your campaign."

"That's bullshit, Beth, Dev's not like that," Billy said.

She mocked him. "'Dev's not like that.' When are you going to grow up, Billy?"

"I don't know why everybody's always picking on Dev," Billy said. "He means well. I know that."

"Poor old Dev. Everybody's friend." Now she was ready for Joan Crawford. She flung an arm in the direction of the door and said, "Get the fuck out of my apartment, Dev. I never want to see you or speak to you as long as I live. And I'll get my own lawyer, thank you very much. Now get out of here."

There wasn't much else to say. In fact, there wasn't anything else to say. I left.

CHAPTER 32

Warren won. The venereal disease played no role. Jim Lake self-destructed one night with a breathtaking racist rant that marked him as at best a rube and at worst a skinhead. I saw a couple of his people the following day. One of them joked that he was on his way to buy a burial plot and casket.

The person I was most wrong about in all this was Warren's wife, Teresa. She'd always seemed to be so unaffected by all the Washington bullshit. But faced with losing her status, she showed us who she really was. The *Post* ran a Style piece a few weeks ago about the returning senators and their spouses. Teresa was shown in a dress by an Italian designer whose name I can neither pronounce nor spell. She was hosting a party for the wives of two new senators, one from each party. She looked very happy. In the background Warren was chatting up a young woman who was undoubtedly on his hunting list.

In the eleven months since I left the campaign, I've never seen any of the principals again. The Cook County state attorney decided against indicting Beth; Laura, whose involvement was apparently un-known to the police, moved to warmer climes; and Kate still works for Warren and dotes on her daughter. Beth and Billy got married a few months back.

I'm back in my apartment. I've spent time in Virginia, Utah, and Florida talking to men and women who are eager to get to Washington and change how this government is run. I've visited my daughter twice and both times took out the lady professor she was telling me about. We had some good times and she'll be here over the holidays. If I promise to put up a tree.

This morning a woman called and said she'd like to talk to me about running for a congressional seat. Very intelligent, very nice voice. The surprise was that Warren had recommended me. I suppose that was my belated reward for not leaking anything I knew about him.

She laughed when she brought up the subject of oppo research. "I don't have anything to hide, Mr. Conrad. I really don't."

"Everybody's got something to hide."

"That's an awfully cynical attitude."

"Yes," I said, "isn't it, though?"